A LOVE FOR ALL SEASONS

Summer's Catch

By Katharine E. Hamilton

ISBN-13: 978-0-578-53687-3

Summer's Catch

www.katharinehamilton.com

Cover Design by Kerry Prater.

To my readers.
You guys helped create Olivia and Matthew.
Thank you for adding a bit of fun to this project.

Acknowledgments

Thank you to everyone who helps a girl out when it comes to putting a book together.

My beta team was awesome. Danielle Pfeil, Megan Wyatt, Alyssa Berry, Sarah Marshall, Glenna Pocock, and Carolyn Rogers. Loved working with you wonderful ladies. Thanks for reading a rough draft and providing valuable feedback on the story. Ramsey thanks you.

Kerry Prater for always whipping up amazing covers for me.

Lauren Hanson for editing for me for what is now our 12th book together.

My family. Because their support is immeasurable.

Brad and Everett, because these two guys hold my heart.

« PROLOGUE »

Strawberries. It was one of the best smells, and most memorable smells, when it came to Oliva Miles. *That and sunscreen*, Matthew mused. The combination of fruity shampoo and sun protectant perfumed the air as he studied the girl of his dreams as she sat beside him on the wooden bench they'd built over the course of the trip. She'd come to visit her grandparents for the entire summer, and he couldn't imagine her leaving Friday Harbor in just a few short hours. She'd be back, of course. Next summer. And the next after that. And so on and so on. But what was he to do all year long? Now that he'd met Olivia, he couldn't begin to understand his life without her. Sure, they were still kids, but without a doubt she was his best friend. And at fifteen, he counted himself lucky, because he'd found the girl he loved.

Dramatic? Maybe. A bit too serious? Possibly. But Matthew didn't care. Olivia Miles was the most beautiful girl he'd ever laid eyes on and she understood him. His parents had given him the lecture already, there was no need to give it to himself.

"Olivia was only here for the summer."

"Don't be so serious. You're only fifteen."

"She's a sweet girl, Matthew, but forever is a long time and you're young."

He'd spilled his heart out to his mother only the night before as she questioned his melancholy attitude. He was sad. Upset. Disappointed that the summer was coming to an end and that he would have to say goodbye to Olivia. His mother had spent the better part of an hour talking him down from a marriage proposal. And yes, he knew it was ridiculous to want to marry a girl at fifteen, but it was the only way he could keep Olivia in Friday Harbor.

The night before he'd taken her out on his sailboat one last time. He'd kissed her then. And, he thought, with quite skill despite it being his first kiss. Olivia claimed it had been her first as well, and he felt good about the bar he'd set should she find herself kissing other guys in the future. Which he doubted would happen since he was set on marrying her. She promised to come back next summer. And they'd keep in touch throughout the year. Letters. Phone calls. None of it would be better than having her here at the harbor, but he'd settle for anything over nothing.

"I have to go," Olivia glanced at the neon pink watch that graced her wrist. "Mom and Dad said we are to ride the afternoon ferry." "I still can't believe you're leaving." She frowned as her blue eyes soaked in the image of the sea one last time from their spot at Lookout Point. "Yeah, me either. I asked Bilbo and Mamie if I could stay here, but—" She shrugged. "I have to go."

Standing, she extended her hand to him and he threaded his fingers through hers and they began the short walk down to the boardwalk. Her sandals tapped against the wooden boards and they immediately dropped hands when her parents came into view. Bilbo, Mamie, his parents, and hers all stood hugging one another as they said their farewells. When Bilbo spotted them, he opened his arms and Olivia raced into them. Everyone would miss her. She was a ray of sunshine that'd settled on the harbor all summer. As her parents began rolling suitcases towards the ferry, Olivia turned, racing back towards Matthew. She stopped a foot away and grinned. "See you next summer, Matthew." He started to reach for her hand and realizing his parents and her grandparents stood watching them, thought better of it. She turned, racing back towards her parents. He jogged after her, hoping to claim a spot on the docks to wave until she disappeared over the horizon. She stumbled, her sandal slipping from her foot. He knelt down and slipped the bedazzled footwear back onto her foot. Looking up, she smiled at him. He'd remember that moment. Her eyes sparkling, the sun behind her golden hair... he'd remember it and cherish it, because deep down he knew he'd never find another girl like Olivia Miles.

« CHAPTER ONE »

June eleventh was the official date. If she'd had a calendar tucked into her suitcase, she would have circled the two ones and then doodled hearts, fireworks, or even an enormous 'x' through that particular day. Despite the lack of physical proof, she earmarked the date in her mind as the significant day in which she, Olivia Miles, had grabbed life by the horns and changed her course. She'd made up her mind. She'd waltzed right into work that day. Brave. Controlled. Confident in the strides she was taking towards changing her life. She knew her boss couldn't possibly take no for an answer. Only he did. Not only did he look at her as if she'd lost her mind, he dismissed her with a wave of his hand and a disappointed shake of his head. And just like that, her nine years in retail management were over.

She'd cried, but only once she was alone in her small apartment with the beautiful view of the brick wall of the neighboring building. She'd questioned her decision of demanding a raise or a transfer, but she still felt she'd earned both. She'd been promised both as well. And when Cheyenne received the promotion and raise instead, Olivia had officially thrown in the towel. Even now, when she was pulling up websites to search for new employment, the disappointment was fading, and relief was settling in its place. There was more to life than working a job in which she had no chance of advancing. She'd hit the proverbial wall, so to speak, and so, in her mind, the only way to go now was up.

She checked her email for the tenth time, waiting for the dismissal paperwork she was sure would be flooding her inbox in a matter of hours. Instead, she found a brief email from her grandmother. Mamie, as Olivia called her, lived amongst the San Juan Islands in Washington— Friday Harbor to be exact— along with Olivia's step-grandfather, Bill. Though no one in the family would call him such a thing. To everyone in the family he was just Bilbo, and he was the only grandfather Olivia had ever known.

Dearest Olivia,
I've been thinking of you. I have a request.
Please call when you can.
Love,
Mamie

Olivia calculated the time difference on her fingers and snatched her phone. She was three hours ahead of them, so she thought she might catch them during their lunchtime.

Bilbo answered on the first ring. "Anchors Aweigh." he greeted.

"Hi, Bilbo." Olivia felt herself smiling as she envisioned his bushy white brows rising in surprise at her voice.

"Well, well, well... how's our favorite Florida gal?"

Grinning, Olivia answered. "Honestly, I could be better."

"What's wrong, Peach?"

She covered the receiver with her palm so as to control her emotions before she started crying all over again. "I lost my job today."

"Oh now," Bilbo sighed. "I'm sorry to hear that. I thought you were up for a promotion?"

"I was. I didn't get it."

"Again?" he asked, knowing the repeated cycle of being passed over she'd dealt with for the last two years.
"Again."

"Well, sweetie, you can't fault yourself for their stupidity."

She snickered. "Thanks, Bilbo. Is Mamie there? She emailed me."

"She's darted over to Leeward's to grab us a couple of boxed lunches right quick, but I know why she emailed you. And by the sounds of it, fate might be on our side."

"What do you mean?"

"Well, your Mamie and I are wanting to travel a bit this summer. We haven't visited family in a while and thought we'd make us a cross country road trip, stopping in on all the family when we pass their directions." She heard him shift the phone on his shoulder and imagined the long, curly cord twisting around his fingers as he talked. "We need someone to man the store for us while we are gone."

"And you thought of me?"

"You were our first pick, Peach."

"Why me? Henry is closer." Her brother lived in Portland, and though it wasn't super close to them, he was certainly in closer proximity than her Orlando, Florida location."

"Well, because you run stores for a living. You know what you're doing. Henry's just an accountant."

She smirked thinking her brother would scoff at being called "*just* an accountant."

"We thought it might be a long shot just because we know how busy you usually are, but perhaps now we might could persuade you. At least until you find something else?"

Olivia gnawed the inside of her cheek as she ran the idea through her head. She was out of a job. She was being offered a job, even if it was just temporary. "For how long?" she asked.

"Through the summer. It is our peak season, so there will be quite a bit of traffic coming through the islands." His tone changed to a persuasive mix of excitement and pride. We'd like to take the summer, until the end of August, to travel."

"I see."

"And you could live here at the house," he continued, his disposition growing cheerier and cheerier as he progressed. "No bills, except for what you might have to keep your place there in Florida. But we'd pay you, of course."

She heard the bell above their shop door jingle and a muffled communication with someone who could only be Mamie coming back with their lunch. "What do you say, Peach?"

"I'm in."

Olivia heard their celebration before Bilbo came back through the line and their excitement carried clear across the country.

"We are so excited." Mamie's voice now hogged the phone. "Can you be here next week?"

"Consider it done," Olivia agreed.

"Oh, Olivia, we can't thank you enough."

"Don't thank me yet. I haven't been to Friday Harbor in years, Mamie. People may not like a stranger working one of the local shops."

"You're not a stranger, sweetie. Why, everyone remembers you."

Cringing at that thought, Olivia just pinched the bridge of her nose. "I'll see you guys next week. Email me the details."

"We will," Bilbo called through the line. "Bye, Peach."

Hanging up, Olivia stared at her cell phone and tried not to let the fear in the pit of her stomach begin to take over. She'd be fine in Friday Harbor. Taking a deep breath, she stood, eyeing her small apartment and limited furnishings. No point in keeping an expensive apartment if she wasn't going to be living in it. And it was Orlando; finding someone to sublease wouldn't be difficult. With a new direction and a new goal in mind, she switched from the employment website to a search for storage facilities. Come next week, she was moving to Friday Harbor.

~

Docking at the Friday Harbor ferry landing was always a bit tight when he wrapped up the lunch cruise. The ferry would be making her way to the dock in a matter of minutes and it was up to him to be unloaded and out of the way before she did. He shifted the cruiser towards the deck and watched as his team unfolded ramps and walkways, tying them to the dock. Hurrying down the steps from the captain's quarters to the landing, Matthew Summers stood and shook hands with all the tourists that waited to thank him for their whale watching adventure. Some wished for a picture with "Captain Matt" before leaving, and he was all smiles until the last of the group had vacated the boat. His team hurried to fold up and lift anchor, and Matt steered their way off the dock and towards an awaiting portside marker reserved for his cruiser. Anchored once more, he removed his captain's hat and placed it on the swiveling chair beside him. He watched as the ferry ship slowly made her way into the harbor. The quiet sounds of waves crashing against the bow had him watching as tourists clambered to their vehicles to ready themselves for exiting. All but one, he noticed. A woman, hair the color of sunshine, stood on the top viewing deck. Her gaze washed over Friday Harbor and landed upon his boat. Though he couldn't tell if she spotted him, he offered a wave in greeting, one she slowly returned by hesitantly lifting her hand. She ducked away then, back into the interior of the ferry, more than likely readying herself to exit. Not everyone who rode the ferry brought their own vehicles, that he knew. Some would leave their cars at the Washington State Ferry Terminal in Anacortes and just use local transportation for their stay, but the numbers were skewed. More and more tourists chose to use their vehicles these days and would thus ride along the ferry with car in tow. He wondered if the blonde woman on the deck would be one of them.

He shuffled along the deck of his boat and picked up loose trash and pamphlets left from his previous tour. He'd prep his cruiser, restock the bathrooms, and then fetch himself a bite to eat at Leeward's before his next tour at two. Glancing at his watch, he was pleased to see he had a couple of hours before embarking on the waters. The ferry would be headed back to Anacortes long before then as well, and he'd have free use of the docks, which he liked. Whistling, he tossed the bag of trash into one of the small dumpsters along the pier and headed up Granny's Way towards lunch. Though the weather hovered in the mid-sixties to low seventies, Matthew found himself drawing in his jacket as he made his way up the shaded street. He stopped in front of Anchors Aweigh as Bill Graves stepped out onto the sidewalk. "Bilbo," he greeted.

The older man's tanned face split into a welcoming smile as his crisp white beard and brows seemed to glow in the sunlight. "Matt. Good to see you, son." The familiar handshake-turned-hug brought a smile to Matt's face as he spotted a set of suitcases by the door. "Going somewhere?" Matt asked.

"Ah." Bilbo shouldered him the rest of the way out of the door and closed it behind him. "Best not say anything in front of Mamie. She's hit the pure fretting stage now." He chuckled. "But, yes, we are going to be doing some traveling this summer."

"But what about the store?" Matt asked.

Bilbo grinned. "Olivia is coming to run the store for us."

"Olivia? Your granddaughter?"

Bilbo beamed at his memory. "Yes, that's the one. You remember her?" His eyes sparkled as he nodded towards the docks. "I'm makin' my way down to the ferry now to pick her up. Want to walk with me?"

"Oh, sure." Matt slipped his hands into his jacket pockets.

Bilbo slapped him on the back as they headed up Granny's Way retracing Matt's previous steps. "I'm sure I shouldn't ask this because I know you're busy this time of year, but if you have a chance every now and then, would you mind checking in on Olivia?"

"Of course." Matt nodded.

"That's a relief." Bilbo waved towards a couple of older men sitting outside the Clam Café as they continued up the street. "She's doing us a big favor coming all the way up here, but it's been a while, you know. And she doesn't really know anyone. Well, apart from you, of course."

"It's been about fifteen years or so, Bilbo, I'd hardly say she knows me," Matt corrected the man.

"Once a friend, always a friend," Bilbo commented as they stepped onto the wooden planks of the pier. "I'm sure she'll remember you. Ah, there she is." Bilbo waved and Matt looked up to find the same blonde woman he'd waved to earlier. She didn't even notice him as her arms flew around Bilbo in a tight hug. The old man, burly and strong, lifted the petite woman off her feet and twirled her in a small circle. When he set her to rights, he motioned towards Matt. "You remember Matthew?"

The woman's smile faltered a bit and Matthew had sudden flashbacks to clumsy, salty kisses on the back of his sailboat. She shook her head and extended a hand. "I'm Olivia."

"Nice to see you again, Olivia. It's been a long time." When he clasped her hand, her right brow slightly rose in recognition. "Matthew... Summers?" she asked. "The sailor?"

His lips twitched into a smile as he nodded and ran a nervous hand over the back of his neck. "That's me."

"Wow." Her blue eyes lit up as she offered him a genuine smile. "It has been a long time. Good to see you."

Bilbo's eyes danced between the two as he watched the young man fidget on his feet and his granddaughter nervously tuck her hair behind her ear. *What memories did the two have of one another*, he wondered? "Well," He clapped his hands together. "Let's get your bags and we'll make it up to the shop before grabbing a bite to eat. Matthew, you'll join us." Bilbo reached for one of the smaller suitcases and Matt took the heavier. Olivia carried her purse and rolled a carry-on behind her. "I didn't realize we'd be walking. I would have packed a lighter case."

"It's not a problem," Matt told her, trying to heft the suitcase over the rough planks of wood. He'd roll it once they reached the street, but for now, it was grit and muscle to carry the thousand pounds of bricks she seemed to have packed with her.

"Your Mamie has us a table reserved over at Leeward's for lunch. You have to make reservations during the busy season if you want to eat in the restaurant due to all the tourists," Bilbo explained. "Don't forget that."

"Got it." Olivia tapped her temple. She looked over to Matthew. "So, what do you do these days? Still sailing?"

"Somewhat. When I can."

"Matthew's the captain of the whale watching ship, *The Voyager*," Bilbo proudly stated.

"Captain?" Olivia asked, her tone impressed. "That must be a neat job."

"Most days."

"That was you then, that waved?" she asked.

"It was. I didn't realize you were someone I actually knew."

She smiled. "After three hours on a ferry, it was nice to see a welcoming person. Thanks for the greeting."

Bilbo opened the door to Anchors Aweigh, a nautical boutique and gift shop housed on one of the busiest streets of Friday Harbor. At their entrance, Mamie squealed, leaving two customers in her wake as she bustled towards them with arms outstretched. "My beautiful Olivia." She swept Olivia into a tight embrace and swayed back and forth until they both giggled. Cupping her granddaughter's face, she kissed her briefly on the nose. "You're even more stunning than I remember. That Florida sun treats you well, I see."

"Most of the time," Olivia replied. "It's good to see you, Mamie."

Mamie squeezed her hand before eyeing Matthew and realizing her husband had commandeered the younger man's muscles for aid in carrying luggage. In sympathy, she brushed a hand over Matthew's arm. "You can just roll that giant bag right on back, Matthew. We have Olivia all set up in the apartment." She pointed for him to follow Bilbo as she linked her arm with Olivia's and led her towards the rear of the shop.

Matthew surveyed the small cottage-style apartment housed in the back of the store. The small door separating the shop from its owner's home was painted a bold turquoise and housed a giant wooden anchor decorated with faux flowers and sailor's rope. The words *Boat Sweet Boat* were etched into the wood, and though there was a price tag attached to it, the anchor served a dual purpose of welcoming Olivia to her new accommodations.

"You'll stay here in the apartment. We figured that'd be best instead of a hotel," Mamie prattled on as she pointed to a corner for Matthew to set the suitcase. Bilbo placed the other bags on the queen bed dressed in white linens. "And since we're leaving this evening, the place is yours starting now anyway." Mamie beamed as she continued to hold Olivia's hand. "Now, why don't we all go grab us a bite to eat. Matthew, you'll join us," she said, repeating her husband's invitation.

"Already ahead of you, dear," Bilbo told her.

"Oh, good." Mamie patted Matthew's shoulder on her way out the door and he and Bilbo brought up the rear. As Mamie began dumping store information onto Olivia, Bilbo hung back long enough to wait for the current customers to mosey out the door before locking it up. He flipped the small sign to *At Lunch* and caught up in stride.

"You'll have to forgive her," Bilbo whispered to Matthew, nodding his head towards Mamie walking in front of them. "She's upset with me for booking us on today's ferry and feels she doesn't have enough time to train Olivia on the store. She's a bit frantic."

"She seems fine to me," Matthew whispered.

"Just wait." Bilbo winked at him as Mamie stopped in her tracks on a gasp. Turning, she faced her husband.

"Why, I just completely walked out on those customers." She held her hands to her cheeks.

"I saw them out, dear," Bilbo reassured her.

Relief washed over her, and her eyes held gratitude as she turned back to Olivia and pulled her onward. Olivia cast one flabbergasted look to her grandfather that didn't go unnoticed by either him or Matthew as Mamie droned on. Bilbo winked at her before she turned back around and began nodding at the appropriate times.

She was small in stature, not much different than she was years ago, but she'd blossomed. And though he hated that term, he couldn't think of a better way to describe it. Olivia was beautiful. Sun-kissed skin and hair, eyes the color of the ocean during high noon, and a smile that did funny things to a man's insides when she fully let it spread. Mamie had been right in her assessment. The Florida sun had definitely treated Olivia with kindness, and he knew, over the next few months, he would as well.

« CHAPTER TWO »

Waving and watching as her grandparents sailed away on the last ferry of the day left her feeling slightly overwhelmed. She'd spent the majority of the afternoon learning about the store, Mamie's methods of running it, and being told which restaurants had the best food, courtesy of Bilbo. The evening wind whipped through her hair and the chill coming off the port had her pulling her jacket tighter. The sun slowly dipped behind the horizon and she heard the sounds of chatter as the last whale watching tour group sailed into the bay in the wake of the ferry.

She'd enjoyed her lunch with Matthew and her grandparents. He was friendly, and he seemed to care deeply for Bilbo and Mamie. She still had a hard time reconciling the teenage image in her head with the man, but the same lopsided grin tilted his lips and made her wish to lightly nudge the opposing corner up to match. He'd laughed when recalling their sailing adventures, but neither spoke of her last evening at Friday Harbor all those years ago. The evening they shared on the back of his hand-me-down sailboat. The picnic. The sunset. The hopes of two young hearts as they discussed how they might convince her parents to let her move to Friday Harbor permanently. Obviously, their plan was faulty. Because not only did Olivia not move to the harbor, she'd never returned. Until now.

The cruiser's horn let out two celebratory blasts as it edged closer to the dock and two men jumped from its decks to secure the rigging. She shielded her eyes against the setting sun and spotted Matthew in the enclosed cabin behind the wheel. He raised a hand in a cheerful wave as he spotted her, and she smiled. She hoped he didn't think she was waiting for him. Feeling a bit unnerved by that thought, she started to walk back towards the shop, but then thought it might be nice to talk to him about his tours. *Tours.* She shook her head in pathetic disgust at herself. No, the real reason she stood and watched him shake hands with strangers and smile for the cameras was that she already felt the crashing wave of loneliness at her grandparents' departure. He waved her over, and several heads turned to see who had caught the handsome captain's eye. Shyly, she walked towards him, her hands in her jacket pockets.

"Welcome back," she greeted.

"Oh, it was just wonderful." An older woman beamed as she bragged about 'Captain Matt' knowing exactly where to steer the ship so they could see *all* the orcas. Olivia bit back a smile as the woman next to her animatedly echoed her friend's sentiments, but with batting eyelashes and friendly pats to Matthew's arm in response.

"Sounds like a fun time." Olivia caught his amused expression as the two women wandered off.

"I'm a hit with the ladies," he whispered.

"I can see that." Olivia nodded towards a handful of other elderly women shuffling along the deck waving to catch his attention before they left.

Chuckling, Matthew lightly punched her shoulder. "And are Mamie and Bilbo off?"

"Just bid them adieu on the last ferry."

"And?"

"And what?"

"How are you feeling?" he asked.

She looked up to find an understanding gaze. Sighing, she answered honestly. "A bit overwhelmed."

He draped an arm over her shoulders and pulled her into a friendly squeeze, releasing her momentarily as he shook hands with departing tourists.

"That's the last of them." His deck hand, Larry, jumped back onto the boat. "I'll start clean up." He nodded a friendly greeting towards Olivia.

"Plans for dinner?" Matthew asked.

"You don't have to entertain me." Olivia shrugged and took a step back towards the shop.

"I didn't think I was. I'm hungry. I was just asking if you were as well. In a roundabout way, I guess." He flashed that quick and ready grin and she felt her insides do a small flip. *Why?* she asked herself. *Why did that smile still have an effect on her after all these years?*

She watched as his crew hurried about the boat gathering trash and rearranging chairs and cushions, setting things to right. "You don't have to," he answered for her. "I just thought since it was your first night on the harbor, you might want to... explore."

"Oh." She turned to him then, realizing she hadn't replied to his invitation and was lost in watching his crew. "No, dinner is fine. You're right, it would be nice to spend my first evening here with... a friend."

He smiled, pleased she accepted. "Good. I've got about a half hour's work left here and I need to move the boat, but I can swing by the shop in an hour or so?"

"Okay." She forced a polite smile, her insides twisting with nerves at the idea of dinner alone with Matthew.

"See ya then." He gave her hair a small tug before hurdling himself over the railing and back onto his ship. His easy familiarity with her calmed her nerves. She watched as he confidently made his way back towards the captain's cabin and she didn't start walking back up the pier until a cold wind slapped her against the face. Shivering, she turned towards home. *Home?* She supposed it was for the next few months, and when she stepped inside the quiet store and to the back apartment with its cozy interior, she had to admit that a sense of home did flood through her, as if her body remembered that summer and the deep longing she had carried for several years afterward. The longing for Friday Harbor to *be* her home. But now, despite the wave of nostalgia, Olivia couldn't envision a future at Friday Harbor. At the moment, and due to life's circumstances, she couldn't envision a life anywhere. Perhaps that was why she so readily accepted Bilbo and Mamie's invitation. She needed to find her place again. And though she never moved to the harbor and her thirteen-year-old heart cracked at never seeing Matthew Summers again, she'd found a path to take. A path that took her to several states and cities, provided for her, and allowed her to live. But a piece of her heart had always remained in Friday Harbor with the lanky, charming boy with the crooked smile. Sighing, Olivia flopped backwards and landed on the white quilt of her bed. She stared at the blades of the ceiling fan until their circular motion hypnotized and the multiple blades merged into one. Lulled to sleep, her dreams carried her back fifteen years to the deck of a small sailboat and the scent of salty air.

~

Matthew patiently waited a few seconds before lightly tapping his knuckles on the storefront glass again. The sign had been flipped for several hours now due to the departure of Bilbo and Mamie, but Olivia was expecting him. He pressed the small button next to the door frame that he knew would ring a doorbell inside the small apartment. He looked up and down the sidewalk as he rocked back and forth on his heels, hands in pockets. He smiled at a few tourists as they passed by and greeted him with excited expressions as they deliberated over where they wished to have dinner. He glanced at his watch. He'd told her he'd swing by in an hour. *Where was she?* He rang the bell once more and saw a shadowy figure approach. The door swung open and a groggy Olivia stood before him. Her hair was tousled and eyes still dreamy as she looked him up and down. "I'm sorry," they stated in unison. Her brows rose curiously. "What are you sorry for?"

"For waking you up." Matthew grimaced.

She ran a hand through her blonde locks, shaking out the tangles. "Oh. Don't feel bad. I didn't mean to fall asleep and shouldn't have. Now I'm probably going to be wide-eyed all night." She stepped out of the store and locked the door. "So where to?"

Matthew turned left. "Do you like chowder?"

"Who doesn't?" Olivia asked.

"Good answer." He grinned. "Pete makes the most amazing clam chowder. Seriously, it'll knock your socks off."

She raised her sandaled foot.

"Sandals, then." He smirked as he pointed. "It's just up this way and around the corner."

"Sounds delicious." She pulled her jacket tighter.

"Cold?"

"A bit. I'm not used to the chilly evenings. Guess I need to toughen up a bit."

"Too much hot sun in Florida, huh?"

"Too much? Nah." Olivia smiled. "Just enough is more like it. When it's not raining."

He opened the door to warmth and the heavy scent of seafood, a scent that encapsulated Friday Harbor. He inhaled a deep breath and released it on a sigh as he heard Olivia do the same. They eyed one another and grinned.

"I love this smell," she told him. "Brings back memories."

"Good ones, I hope." He tucked his hands into his pockets again as they waited at the hostess stand to be seated.

"All my memories of Friday Harbor are good ones," she answered.

"Even when it comes to an awkward teenage boy?"

"Especially those."

His lips quirked as the hostess walked up and grabbed two menus and waved them onward. "I always wondered. I wasn't sure if you'd remember me," he murmured as they walked.

"Why? That was a good summer. One of the happiest for me."

"Really?" Matthew asked, his right brow arching into his sun-kissed hairline.

She chuckled at his doubtful expression. "Yes, really. Is that so hard to believe?"

"Well, yeah, it kind of is. I mean..." He fidgeted with his napkin and silverware. "You never came back."

Nodding, she stared at him a long, silent minute and then leaned forward as if to share a secret. "I'm sorry for that."

He cleared his throat and leaned back to allow the waitress to set two glasses of water before them. Matthew held up two fingers as he pointed to the special sign and the woman hurried away. "You have nothing to be sorry for. We were young."

"But I promised." Her blue eyes sparkled as she shook her head in disdain at her actions.

"You were thirteen, Olivia. Sometimes things are out of our hands. Besides, I was only fifteen. We were just kids. Dreamers. What did we think would happen? That you'd move to Friday Harbor and we could be together forever?" He smiled at the memory. The memory of them on the back of his beat-up sailboat. Her cutoff shorts and bikini top, complete with bedazzled sandals, much like the ones she currently wore. And his faded t-shirt over cargo shorts that housed various flies and baits for fishing. She was beautiful then, and she was even more beautiful now. But life had seasoned them both. Ups and downs had left their marks, whether physical or emotional, and sweet summer promises between two teenagers did not hold much weight in the grand scheme of life.

"I guess you're right," she sighed. "I am sorry though. We had such… innocence about it all."

"That we did." He grinned as two bowls of creamy chowder were set before them. In unison, they both leaned over their bowls and took a deep inhale.

"So, fill me in then," she said, as she grabbed her spoon and began stirring her meal.

"On what?"

"The last fifteen years." She laughed as his eyes widened. "What has Matthew Summers been up to? Are you married? Seeing someone? Have kids? You're obviously a boat captain now. Do you still sail?"

He took a bite of his chowder and waited until her rapid-fire questioning died down. "No. No. No. And yes."

She tilted her head and rolled her eyes. "Really? That's all you're going to give me? I mean, at least tell me what made you decide to guide the orca tours."

He shrugged. "It was an opportunity that fell into my lap. Turns out I enjoyed it. Stuck with it. And here I am now."

A trace of annoyance washed over her face before she lowered her eyes back to her chowder. It wasn't that he was trying to be vague, it was just there wasn't much to his story. It was really that simple, but he could see her attempts at trying to connect and felt a sudden wash of regret at not giving her more of an explanation and decided to try a bit harder. "A young guy, about our age, used to run the tours. His wife was from Portland. Her father fell ill, and they decided to visit Oregon for a couple of weeks. He asked me to run the tours while he was gone. Up to that point, I was just a fisherman, working on various crews. I'd also take a few tourists sailing every now and then. Well, when they visited Portland, they decided they wanted to stay. He offered me the business."

"And you enjoy it?"

"Oh, I love it." He beamed. "I love sharing about the orcas, but also just about the San Juan Islands. People come here for an escape and a good time. I do my best to give it to them. Plus, I love being on the water."

"That hasn't changed at least. I will have to catch one of your tours while I'm here."

"Yes. You will. In fact, I'll even let you ride in the captain's seat."

She placed a hand over her heart and gasped. "Why, that sounds like a dream come true."

He laughed at her sarcasm and tossed an oyster cracker at her. She giggled as she dropped it into her chowder. "I would love to ride along, though. I remember the orca tour when we came that summer. That was the second time I'd been on a tour, but for some reason it was more magical the second time. Probably because I was older and could appreciate it more. It would be neat to experience it as an adult now."

"Just let me know when. I'll pick you up." He winked. "So, tell me about you. What made you decide to come all this way after so long?"

"Bilbo and Mamie needed me," she stated simply. "And my job... well, let's just say I parted ways with the company, so I was free."

"Sorry to hear that."

Shrugging, she nudged her empty bowl to the edge of the table for the waitress to swing by and retrieve. "Don't be. It's for the best. I'd reached my max potential there. I was passed over for promotion after promotion and they made it clear I wouldn't be receiving one any time soon. So... here I am."

"Have you been in Florida all this time?"

A cloud descended over her face. "No. My mom, Henry, and I moved quite a bit after... well, that summer. She ended up settling in Sarasota when I was eighteen and still lives there. She's remarried now. Great guy named Tim. I moved to Orlando a couple of years ago from New Orleans.

I've sort of hopped around with my company. Wherever they needed me, I went."

"I was sorry to hear about your parents."

She sighed. "Yeah." Her eyes drifted over the crowded diner and then back to him. "It was one reason I never came back here. Friday Harbor was the last place we were ever really a family. It was only a month after that when my dad left. I think it was too hard for my mom to come back here. And well… I didn't want to leave her after it all happened and after the divorce. So, I just stayed. Wherever she went, I followed."

"I can understand that. It's hard for a thirteen-year-old to fly across the country by themselves. Well, *then* it was."

"Time passes quicker than you realize. When Bilbo asked me to come, it seemed like only yesterday that I was here. And when I arrived," She smiled. "All the familiar sights and smells. It was like waking up from a long sleep and feeling like I was finally home. And you, wow, you look exactly the same."

"Lord, I hope not," he laughed.

"I meant more mature, obviously." She grinned. "When I saw you smile, I immediately knew who you were."

"Then why'd you act like you didn't?" he countered.

"Well, it did take me a few seconds after seeing you again to register it was actually you. But the smile gives it away."

"Must be a good one," he teased.

"It is."

Her compliment kicked him back a step as he observed the seriousness in its delivery. She smiled warmly as the waitress approached their table and rested the small black folder on the edge, their bill nestled inside. Matt reached for it. "My treat."

"Don't be silly. I owe you a meal."

"For what?"

"Oh, let's see. For breaking my promise fifteen years ago. For you looking out for my grandparents all these years. And if that's not enough, then for lugging my heavy suitcases up the docks and to the shop."

He snapped and pointed at her. "Now that one is definitely worth a free bowl of chowder."

Laughing, she slipped her credit card into the folder and handed it to the waitress.

"I'm not mad at you, you know. For breaking the promise. It was a long time ago, Liv." The old nickname slipped off his tongue so easily as he watched her cheeks flush at his intimacy.

"I know you're not. It's just... it was important to me. At the time," she quickly added. "And it was my word. I don't like people thinking I'm not a woman of my word. And I broke it with you. That was the last memory you have of me."

"Not true," he said. "My last memory of you is your blonde ponytail bouncing up the docks towards the ferry. You stumbled on the uneven boards and lost your flip flop. I bent down to help you put it back on since your hands were full. I looked up, the sun shining behind you, and your hair was radiant, but your eyes—" He held a palm to his chest and acted as if an arrow had shot through his heart.

She laughed.

"They were like the ocean. So blue and clear. That image stayed with me for a while," he admitted. "That's my last memory of you."

"Even when I didn't call or write or come back?"

"Even then. When I thought about Olivia Miles, all I saw was radiance."

She looked away, her gaze suddenly sad. "You're sweet to say that."

"And I mean it." He reached forward and squeezed her hand, surprising her. Her sparkly blue gaze looked back at him. "Besides, you're here now, so it would seem," He stood and waited for her to stand as well. "you have not broken your promise."

Scoffing at the thought, she allowed him to escort her outside. "Just fifteen years behind schedule," she retorted.

"True. But you *did* come back. What's that saying... Better late than never?" He looked down at her and winked as he opened the door and they stepped out onto the boardwalk.

« CHAPTER THREE »

Holding her hands to the small of her back, Olivia stretched and arched to try and work out the new aches and pains that had crept up on her as the day wore on. She'd been sifting through Mamie's storage room, organizing unboxed merchandise and random finds into assigned shelf spaces. She also decided to take on the layout and display of the store. Mamie did say she could make any changes she wanted while she was here, so Olivia decided to spruce up the store's floor design. It was, after all, her area of expertise. But she also knew she was only one person, the *only* person to work the store, so her work was done in small increments. She'd hidden in the back room and worked most of the afternoon, only venturing out onto the sales floor when she heard the bell above the door jingle, announcing that she had customers. She counted the day as a great first day of work. She'd sold an expensive glass mobile of circulating dolphins and whales, several outfits to a woman who'd lost her luggage on her flight to Seattle and made the trip on the ferry any way, and various small tokens of San Juan Islands tourist buys. She wasn't sure what counted as a good day in sales but made a mental note to look at Mamie's numbers again to see how the day compared to the usual.

Glancing at her watch, she felt relief in knowing she could now flip the sign on the front door and continue her work in peace. Her plans to rearrange the area around the register could only be done while the store was closed because she planned to make a mess. A *necessary* mess. She'd been setting aside boxes throughout the day and removing items from around the sales floor to move towards the cash-wrap. As she flipped the sign, she spotted Matthew up the walkway talking with a man dressed in typical island-wear complete with a floppy fisherman's hat. For all she knew, the man could very well be a fisherman, and Matthew would definitely know him due to his former work. His eyes darted to her door and she paused in turning the sign over. He held up a hand for her to wait, and the man turned to see what had caught his attention. They said their farewells and Matthew jogged the remaining distance to her door. "Locking me out?" The charming smile that she was sure brightened anyone's day flashed as he stepped into the store and allowed her to lock up behind him.

"It's quittin' time, Summers." Olivia turned at the sound of his surprise.

"Whoa. What happened in here?" He turned to her with wide eyes. "Mamie would have a heart attack."

Smiling, Olivia rested her hands on her hips. "That's why it's taking place while she's not here. I'm doing a bit of rearranging."

"I'll say."

"Just trying to make the most of what she has. Some areas of the store just don't make sense. Like these paperweights for example." She held up a glass orb that showcased blown glass orcas on the inside. "I sold three today, but I probably could have sold more if they were up towards the front of the store near the register. They're not super expensive. They're keepsakes, and they're cute. People will buy them on impulse or as an add-on, so they should be up here, not scattered around the store."

"Logical." He nodded in agreement.

"And shot glasses, and magnets, and beaded necklaces." She motioned towards the remaining boxes nestled next to the checkout.

"It's smart, but don't the other shops sort of do that?"

"Probably," Olivia admitted. "It's sort of a gimmick."

"Do you think that's why Mamie *doesn't* do it? To be different?"

"No. I honestly think she just sticks stuff where she finds a place. There truly is no rhyme or reason to this place. It's just stuff all crammed in here together. It's a bit overwhelming."

"I can agree with that as well." He chuckled as he looked around.

"So, how was your day?" she asked.

"Pretty good. Had a kid get sick on the last tour. Couldn't handle the waves. Thank goodness for Larry. He cleaned it up faster than you could have blinked."

"Yikes. Yeah, that's definitely not a glamorous job."

"Neither is this." He pointed at the dust that coated the front of her shorts and shirt.

"Oh, right. Well, I was also organizing their storage room. Trying to see what inventory they have and what I could bring out. My goal is to blow all their previous sales records out of the water this season. Earn my keep, so to speak."

"I have no doubts that you will."

"So, what brings you by my work in progress?"

Turning, his warm gaze traveled over her and flutters settled in her stomach. "Was going to steal you away for supper again tonight, but it looks like we will be dining in. Pizza work for you?"

Olivia tilted her head and scrupulously surveyed him. "You plan on helping me?"

"Sure. Why not?"

"It's a pretty big project."

"I can handle it." He winked at her and she dropped her hands from her hips and walked towards the phone. "Who do I call for pizza?"

"That's the spirit." He clapped his hands, rubbing his palms together as he snatched the phone out of her hands. "I'll do this, and you think of where you want to put me to work."

"Alright." She squinted her eyes as she contemplated his sincerity.

"What?"

"You sure you want to help me? I'm a bit... overzealous when it comes to this stuff."

Laughing, he held up his finger as he began speaking into the receiver. "Jake, hey, it's Matt. I need some pizzas... Yes, the usual... only make it two. And I'm at Anchors Aweigh... Got it. Thanks." He hung up and set the phone in the receiver. "Yes, I want to help you. I think it will be fun to surprise Mamie and Bilbo with a makeover."

"Well, okay then, first things first." She pointed towards the front of the store. "I want to change out the window displays. It's now summer and Mamie still has heavier clothing items showcased."

"Well, the mornings and evenings are still a bit chilly. Wouldn't it make sense to leave them there?"

"No." Olivia began removing the hanging items from the rack and transferring them to a rolling rack she could move about the store. "We are now moving into a season where tourists want to think of sun and sea, not winter garb. We will use a few of the lighter weight cardigans and sweaters as layering pieces, but for the most part, we want the window to appeal to summer vacationers. They're arriving now and looking to shop."

Matthew stared at her.

"What?"

He shook his head and smiled. "I'm just impressed. You seem to really know what you're doing."

"Well, this *is* what I do for a living." Her tone held no offense, but she wondered why it came to such a surprise to him.

"Right. Well, where do you want me? Or what can I do?"

She pointed to a set of wall shelves behind the front window. "I want all of that merchandise taken down and moved to that table for now." She motioned towards the back of the store. "And then you can take down the shelves and the faux wall they are screwed into. We want it to feel open and want the customers inside the store to still be able to see outside."

"Got it. That I can do." Stepping up onto the platform of the window display, he grabbed the first few breakable items and carefully carried them across the store as Olivia continued her work of removing the clothing and furniture pieces nestled on the platform.

"So, how's your brother?" Matthew asked. "He still living in Portland?"

Hefting a small end table, Olivia grunted before replying. Matthew hurried towards her and helped her shift it out of the way. Taking a relieved breath, she swiped her bangs out of her eyes. "He's good. And yes, still in Portland. He married two years ago and has his first child on the way." Smiling, she walked back towards the window. "He's an accountant."

"I remember Bilbo telling me that one time."

"He seems to love it."

"And your mom? How's she?"

"Oh, she's good. Tim is an avid golfer and they live in an exclusive country club community where she's able to brush elbows with Sarasota's elite and Tim can golf to his heart's content. They're happy."

"And your dad?"

She paused, not sure what to say about her dad. After he'd left them, she went years not speaking with him. Though they'd somewhat patched up their relationship, Olivia couldn't say she really knew him all that well anymore. "He lives in New Orleans, runs a touristy t-shirt shop on Magazine Street."

"Glad to hear you still keep in touch with him." His voice turned serious and had her glancing his direction.

"I'll admit our relationship isn't the best, but he's my dad. I'm trying. And so is he. Some days are easier than others."

"Sometimes that's all you can do is take it one day at a time."

"What about you? Your parents still live around here?"

"Yep, up in Lakedale. My dad handles boat rides back and forth from the resort and my mom retired a couple of years ago and stays at home. They're happy. He sails any day the sun is out and most of the time Mom's on the boat with Dad. But they're doing well."

"That's good. I vaguely remember them." Olivia saw the pizza delivery man before he knocked and walked towards the door and unlocked it.

The handsome man's eyebrows bounced up in surprise when he saw her. "Delivery for Matt." He dragged out the name as if he were uncertain whether he was at the right place.

"Hey, Jake," Matthew called from behind her. Olivia stepped out of the way so the man could enter. His face split into a smile as he saw his friend. "This is Olivia. She's Mamie and Bilbo's granddaughter."

"Olivia? As in *the* Olivia?" Jake's eyes bounced from Matt to her and she tilted her head in curiosity at his question.

"Um, yeah." Matt's face flushed as he nodded for Jake to set the pizzas on the register counter.

"Wow, man I've heard a lot about you." Jake extended his hand and Olivia responded with a shake.

"I hope it's all been good."

Jake's smile turned mischievous as he eyed Matt over the top of Olivia's head. "Oh, it has. It definitely has, but it's nice to see the real woman is as beautiful as the one I had imagined."

It was Olivia's turn to blush as she motioned towards the pizza. "So, what do we owe you?"

Matthew shouldered past her and handed his friend money. "I've got this round." He all but nudged Jake towards the door as his friend continued to smile at Olivia.

"You know, you should come to Ramsey's on Friday night," he called to her as he stepped out the door. "You'd be a hit."

"Okay, go on now." Matthew lightly shoved Jake's shoulder.

"What is Ramsey's?" Olivia held the door open and waited for Jake to respond.

Seeing Matthew's discomfort had Jake enjoying the moment a bit longer. "Just a hole in the wall bar over behind the docks. Our buddy, Ramsey Jenkins, owns it."

"It's just a bunch of fishermen that hang out after work," Matthew told her. "Not exactly the finest establishment."

"Hey now, I hang out there." Jake feigned offense and Olivia grinned. "Seriously, you should come if you're in town for the week."

"I'm here all summer," Olivia explained.

Jake's smile spread even further, showcasing a dazzling white smile set in a lean, tanned face. His brown eyes sparkled. "Even better. You definitely have to come and meet everyone. Matt, make it happen." He pointed a finger at Matt before shoving it into his pocket. "I've got to get back, but I will see you Friday, Olivia." He winked as he nodded a farewell to Matt over her shoulder and whistled as he walked up the boardwalk.

Olivia closed the door and smiled. "He seems nice."

Matthew walked towards the pizza boxes and opened one of the lids. "Jake's a good friend. We've known each other since we were boys."

"Was he here the last time I was here?"

"Yes. Though you probably won't remember him. Not sure if you two ever met. Back then he helped his parents at the Lakedale Resort. His mom was the manager."

"Ah. I see. Didn't think I recognized him."

"And listen," Matt held up his hand in warning. "Ramsey's is fun, but just a fair warning to you... not many women hang out there."

"So, are you saying I shouldn't go?" Olivia asked, concern etching her face.

"No. Yes. Maybe. I don't know." He ran a hand through his hair. "I'm just saying that it's not every day that a... well, a pretty female walks in the door at Ramsey's, so just... you might want to be prepared to be hit on. I mean, you should be fine if you're with me, but I can't make any promises. These are some rough and tumble kind of men who mostly spend their time on the water. Their manners are a bit... brusque."

"Do you want me to go?" She studied him as he turned back to the pizza, his shoulders relaxed, his brown hair streaked by the sun ruffled on top by his busy hands. When he turned, his hazel eyes held warmth and trepidation. "I'd love for you to come."

"Really?"

"Really. Just don't say I didn't warn you. And if it gets to be too much, just tell me and we can leave. It won't hurt my feelings if you don't enjoy my friends."

"So, these people are all your friends?" she asked.

"Well, not all of them, but some of them, yes. I *know* all of them, but not *all* of them are what I'd consider my friends, ya know? Though my friends *will* be there, and—"

"Matthew," She giggled as she reached out and grabbed his arms. "Calm down. I get it. Some are your friends, but all are local acquaintances. And

I'm sure they are all great in their own way. I look forward to it."

He relaxed again and smiled as he handed her a slice of pizza.

"By the way, what did Jake mean by '*the* Olivia'?"

Matthew sputtered as he tried to swallow his pizza and avoid choking at the question she just asked him. Concern had her stepping forward, but he held up his hand and warded her off by taking a step towards the back room to finish coughing and to grab a soda out of the mini fridge he knew Bilbo stocked back there.

When he returned, she let the matter rest and found herself quite pleased that his friends would know of her even though she'd been absent for so many years. Perhaps the funny feelings she'd been having since being back on Friday Harbor weren't completely one-sided. Or perhaps, her thoughts turning darker, they knew her as the girl who broke his heart all those years ago. And perhaps, that was one reason Matthew was hesitant in taking her to Ramsey's. Her initial excitement over the idea began to wane as she watched Matt work with one hand while eating his pizza with the other. Shoving her shoulders back, she walked back towards the window display and began removing more merchandise. There only one way to find out what sort of reputation '*the* Olivia' had. Fueled with determination and a small spark of excitement, Olivia caught Matthew's amused gaze as she hoisted a large planter over her head and carried it towards the back. She felt him watching her and prayed she wouldn't trip over the various objects she'd scattered about the store, but as she turned the corner to the store room, she misjudged an extended shelf and the sound of shattering glass had her squealing and groaning in frustration as Matthew's footsteps hurried towards her.

~

"Oh no! Now look what I've done!" She sat the planter down with a crunch as it landed on various shards of glass. Matt waited to see what her next move would be and whether he should help her or not. "I can't believe I broke all these— well— these... *things*. These— *What* exactly are *these*?" She motioned towards the ground and Matthew threw his head back and laughed. She grinned as she cautiously stepped through the rubble on the floor and back towards him. "Seriously though, what in the world are those?"

"Creepy orca clowns?" He looked down at her and she crossed her eyes which only made him laugh harder.

"Why would Mamie even consider having these weird things in her store?"

Matthew bent over as his laughter continued, resting his hands on his knees. "I don't know, but they've been here for years."

"Years?!"

"Stop it." He held a hand to his heart as he tried to contain his hysterics. "Your face—" He tried to mimic the disgusted look she wore from staring at the disturbing figurines.

"Matthew, be honest with me." She placed her hands on her hips and narrowed her eyes. "Have they really been here for *years*?" Her lips twitched as she watched him attempt to compose himself.

He nodded. "Oh yeah. At *least* since I was eighteen or so."

"*That* long?! Geez! Then I did us all a favor. Wow." She shook her head. "Mamie, Mamie, Mamie..."

He inhaled a deep breath on a sigh as he was finally able to stop laughing.

"Why didn't she just ship them back to the supplier when they didn't sell?"

"You are asking the wrong person. All I know is that I always avoided this part of the store because I knew they were hiding somewhere on the shelves."

"They've even been in the same location all this time? Does Mamie not rearrange the store that often?"

"Um, no. New stuff comes in and goes towards the front and then whatever doesn't sell just gets mixed in with the rest. Nothing like the huge rotation that you're doing."

"Wow. A store should have a fresh floor set every six weeks or so."

"Well, now that you're here maybe you can introduce them to some change."

"I'm officially more determined now that I know there are creepy orca clowns from thirteen years ago *still* on the shelf."

He bit back a laugh and she grinned knowing he wanted to. He opted for sobriety. "So, I'll get the broom and start sweeping the 'creepy orca clowns' up. You finish what you started up front."

"Thanks." She patted his arm on her way by him and back to the front of the store.

As he swept, he listened to the movements of merchandise, her light humming of what sounded like a Beatles song, and a few grunts as she lifted heavy items. Smiling to himself, he still couldn't believe Olivia Miles was back in Friday Harbor and that he stood in the small shop where he'd first met her in fifteen years ago. As far as growing up, Olivia seemed like a nice woman with a level head on her shoulders. He knew she kept in touch with Bilbo and Mamie throughout the years due to Bilbo's annual reports after the holidays. Truth be told, Matt loved those reports. He loved hearing what Olivia was up to, what all she'd accomplished. He also dreaded the day Bilbo would mention her marrying and settling down, but he never did. Not that Matt expected to pick up where he and Olivia had left off all those years ago, but he'd be lying if he didn't admit he was glad she was back in the harbor. Though they'd been young the last time she was here, he remembered every moment they spent together. And if a kid could lose his heart at fifteen, he had. And he'd yet to fully recover from her departure all those years ago.

Oh, he'd dated here and there over the years. Had a few relationships. But nothing serious. He only wanted one person back then. Olivia. And when it looked as if she were never coming back, it was then he finally started dating around. That was at nineteen. He'd never come close to marrying anyone, because a piece of him left when she hopped the ferry and disappeared. Maybe it was his childish heart that hopped aboard and sailed away with her and left in its place a hopeful heart that was to face emotional bruising as her absence grew longer. That was exactly what happened, anyway. And though he'd been fifteen, he'd loved her. He smirked to himself at the thought of his younger self being helplessly and hopelessly in love. He'd dissected those feelings over the years. Did he truly love Olivia back then? Can a fifteen-year-old really even know what love was? His answers continued to be 'yes.' As he grew older, he had tried to convince himself it was a foolish notion but always failed. Over and over again, he failed. He'd loved Olivia. And he had wished for years for her to return to the harbor. To him.

Now, he treaded carefully. He didn't stay in relationships long enough to really nurture love. Rather, he quite avoided it. Not that he didn't want it. He did. He just wasn't quite sure if he wanted to be blind to it like he was then. Even when he knew it was ridiculous to pine away for Olivia, he had. For four years. *Four years!* And she haunted him even to this day. When he first saw her on the ferry, not knowing who she was, it was the first time he'd been taken aback by someone other than her. Only it *was* her. Only an adult her. And so, her spell over him continued. Olivia Miles was the only girl to ever bewitch him. Her masterful spell: sincerity. She'd always been sincere and kind. That he *did* remember. And from what he'd seen so far in the couple of days she'd been back, her words, motives, and actions reflected the same unchanged demeanor. He heard another calamitous crash and stifled a laugh as he poked his head around the corner. "You okay?" he called.

"Yes." He heard an exasperated huff. "My rolling rack collapsed. No big deal."

"Need some help?"

"No, I've got it. Thanks."

He knelt to sweep the remaining pieces of glass into the dustpan and dumped it into the trash. He nudged the shelving unit a bit off its mark so as to allow more room should they need to carry any other items to the storeroom. Satisfied, he walked towards the front.

"Wow." He rested his hands on his hips impressed with her work.

"The idea is to create scenes," she explained, not looking up as she maneuvered a leaf-patterned cushion onto an old wooden Adirondack chair that sat angled next to a wrought iron patio table. She'd dressed two mannequins in the layered outfits she'd spoken of earlier and posed them as spectators around the patio scene. She then situated various items, creating an entire story for passersby. "So, this scene will have more of an outdoor feel to it. Then over there—" She pointed to an area she'd already established with a large rectangular rope rug. "That's where we are going to cultivate more of a blue area. There are some great pieces in here that could really play off one another if they were just *near* one another. You know?"

"I do *not* know, but it is obvious that you do. I think it looks great."

She smiled, swiping a hand over her forehead to remove the small beads of sweat that rested there. "I've drafted a few ideas over there." She pointed to the register and walked towards her papers as he followed. He perused her sketches.

She looked up at him expectantly. "Well? What do you think?"

"I think it's going to look great." He wasn't sure how to respond due to his lack of vision. He needed to see it finished. He couldn't envision the store based on sketches; he just didn't have the same eye she had for design. But he could tell his lack-luster reply dampened her spirits. "Honestly, this looks like a great plan. I'm just not one who can envision what you do. But," he added with a wide smile. "I'm eager to see it all come together."

She exhaled a pent-up breath that had her feathered bangs fluttering. "We've got work to do then, if I'm to show you my skills."

He playfully nudged her. "You already have in the window display."

Horror stamped itself across her face as she shook her head. "I'm not even done with that. It looks terrible so far."

Shaking his head, he turned her shoulders back towards the front of the store and pushed her towards her work. "Then I guess you better step up your game, Liv." Satisfied when he heard a light giggle, he set about moving items out of her 'blue' section to make room for whatever she longed to place there. He noticed her eagle eye as he worked. The constant surveillance. The not exactly hovering, but attentive oversight required to make sure he was following her plans. She worked quietly, only pitching in suggestions or asking opinions here and there, and though he longed for more personal conversation to learn more about her, he appreciated her work ethic and seeing her pour her talents into Bilbo and Mamie's shop. She loved them, and it was evident in the care she took with each piece she surveyed and placed. Each random knick-knack that Mamie had collected over the years that lingered hidden in a dark corner or crowded shelf was given new life in the hands of Olivia. And though, as he glanced at his watch, it was almost nine and his usual turning in time, he wished to keep helping her just to say he was part of what would be a phenomenal transformation. He saw her yawn and then shake her head as if sleep were an uninvited guest and she didn't have time for the nuisance.

"So, at what point do you call it a night?" he asked.

Her head popped up from the colored gems she was placing in a crystal bowl. "Once the store is somewhat navigable for tomorrow's workday. You fading on me?"

"It's about that time for me, I'm afraid. My mornings start a bit early. I'm fishing in the morning."

"Fishing for work or pleasure?" she asked.

"Work. Handy was short a man this week, so he asked me to fill in."

Worry etched her forehead. "I didn't realize. You should have told me. You're probably exhausted after having to fish and then captain your tours and now this."

"Don't worry about it."

"Matthew—"

"Don't Matthew me. Besides, most people call me Matt now. I wanted to help you. I also do not want to leave you with this mess."

"I'm just going to move a few more things and then I will be done, so you can head out. I'm wrapping up."

"You sure?"

"Definitely." She started walking towards the door and unlocked it to the quiet sounds of waves crashing softly against the pier. "I appreciate you helping me."

"Anytime. I've enjoyed it." He stepped out and turned to bid a final farewell as the lights from the store glistened off her bright hair. He remembered toying with her ponytail on the back of his very first boat, that sunny smile that looked up at him with excitement and adoration. He wondered if her hair was as silky now as it was then. He blinked, realizing she'd been speaking to him.

"You falling asleep on your feet?" She chuckled as she leaned against the door.

Clearing his throat and forcing a smile, he nodded. "I guess so. I'm leaving now. It's... It's good to have you back, Liv," he said, his tone serious as he watched a light flush dance its way up her neck and to her cheeks.

"Thanks. Matt." she added, testing out his requested moniker.

His lips twitched in response and he started down the boardwalk, hands in his pockets, and a bouncy blonde ponytail in his mind.

« CHAPTER FOUR »

"I'm up!" Olivia jolted awake, her head rested on folded arms as her mind cleared and she realized the store's telephone was ringing. She sat in one of the oversized vintage chairs she'd pushed against the back wall of the blue scene she'd last been working on. She shuffled her way towards the chair behind the register counter and answered.

"Anchors Aweigh."

"Hi, Peach." Bilbo's cheerful tone brought a smile to her face.

"Morning, Bilbo."

"Morning?" he asked. "Has it been that busy of a day?"

Olivia glanced at the clock and stifled her gasp as she realized it was already close to lunchtime and she had yet to open the store. She quickly placed the receiver on the counter and ran to flip the sign and unlock the door. When she slid back into the chair and held the phone to her ear, Bilbo was sharing he and Mamie's early adventures.

"So, what about you?" He asked. "You learning your way around the store well enough?"

"You could say that." She bit back a smile as she thought of the mess she'd created yesterday and last night. She now knew the shop inside and out.

"Be sure to have a little fun while you're there."

"I will. I'm actually going to Ramsey's tonight with Matt."

"Really?"

"Yep."

"Well, that's good, Peach. You just be sure to stick close to Matthew. Depending on the crowd, Ramsey's can get a bit rowdy."

"Matt has already warned me," she chuckled. "And Jake as well."

"Ah, Jake. He's a good kid."

She laughed thinking of the tall, fully grown man she'd met last night and the fact Bilbo still called him a kid. "He seemed nice."

"He and Matt are as thick as thieves. Always have been. They'll look after you."

"I don't need to be looked after, Bilbo."

"Of course you do. Everyone needs someone to keep an eye on them. Heavens, could you imagine if I didn't have Mamie looking after me? Why, I'd be a clumsy fool."

Snickering, Olivia sighed as she leaned back in the chair and rested her feet on the counter. The bell above the door jingled and Matt walked inside with two Styrofoam containers fragranced with spices that had her mouth watering. "Hey there," Matt greeted and then grimaced when he saw the phone to her ear. She plopped her feet to the floor.

"Yes, Matt just walked in with some lunch."

"Oh good. Give him my best. You two have a good day. Thanks for helping out, Peach. You're the best."

"As are you, Bilbo. Love you. Bye." She hung up and smiled up at Matt. "I love when a man comes bearing gifts."

He laughed as he handed her a carton. "Nice to see you awake."

Her face blanched. "I fell asleep over there." She pointed to the bright turquoise chair. "I feel so bad. The store should have been opened hours ago."

"Well, if it makes you feel any better, I don't think you would have had many people venturing in anyway. A storm blew in pretty early this morning and is just now starting to clear. I've canceled all my tours today because of it, and there aren't many people milling about."

Relieved, she stood, carton in hand. "That does make me feel better. Thanks for telling me. Want to eat over in this section?" She pointed to the turquoise chair and the small sitting area she'd created with nautical nets featured on the walls above a pale blue sofa with anchor-embroidered pillows and a captain's wheel glass-topped table in the middle with various bowls of trinkets and figurines.

"Wow. I thought you were wrapping it up last night?"

"I did... Just five hours later." She grimaced when he narrowed his eyes at her. "I couldn't stop. I was on a roll."

"Well, it looks fantastic. Not as cluttered, though I see everything that was once here. I don't know how you did it."

"Thanks. I'm taking today off and will start the next change up on Sunday when the store is closed. I'm hoping tomorrow will be a busier day since it's the weekend."

"Should be. I'm booked all day. Four orca tours and three sailing trips."

"Wow. That is a busy day."

"Want to come on a tour?"

She waved her hands around the store. "I have to be here."

"My mom could come watch the store for a bit. She's helped Bilbo and Mamie in the past. She wouldn't mind watching it for a few hours."

Olivia nibbled her bottom lip as she considered.

"First tour of the morning so you could be back the rest of the day?" he prodded. "Captain Matt's special guest." He winked as she laughed.

"How could I refuse that?"

"Great. I'll swing by here in the morning with Mom."

"You sure she won't mind?"

"Not at all. She'd probably help more if you need her to. She enjoys it."

"I might take her up on that in the next few months, just so I can work on rotating stock more. I'd like to change things up periodically, but it's hard to man the floor when I'm digging around in the back room."

"Seriously, you should propose the idea to her tomorrow. She'd love to help."

"I definitely will. And thanks for this." She pointed her fork at her lunch of shrimp linguini. "What do I owe you?"

"Nothing."

"Matt," She looked heavenward on a sigh. "You've bought me multiple meals already."

"I bought pizza. You bought chowder. I bought this. You can foot the bill at Ramsey's tonight. How's that?"

"You're still okay with me going?"

"Why wouldn't I be?"

"Just seemed like you weren't too keen on the idea last night." She shrugged her shoulders before taking another bite of her lunch.

"It wasn't that I didn't want you to go. It's just... I want you to go." His purposeful avoidance of an explanation had her brows rising, but he offered no further comment, so she let the matter drop.

"I'm looking forward to it. What time should I be ready?"

"I can come by about nine, if that works for you?"

Nodding, she set her carton on the table and rested her head against the back of the chair. "This really is a comfortable chair."

He laughed. "Must be if you slept in it all night."

Her lips tilted into a tired smile. "Is it bad that I'm hoping it will be a slow day so I can just sit here and possibly read?"

"That's what your Mamie does," he replied. "She and Bilbo both. You walk in and one of them is setting down a book to stand and greet customers."

"I noticed they had quite a selection of books. I might do that."

"You should. It will help you rest you up for tonight."

He stood and carried both their containers to the trash bin. Glancing at the clock above the register, he turned with a regretful frown. "I've got to head out. Though I don't have tours today, I'm still on the water with Handy."

Olivia walked him to the door. "Thanks for stopping by and keeping me company." She ran a hand through her hair and let it fall, suddenly aware that she hadn't showered from the day before and still wore the previous day's clothes. Confidence fled as Matt's steady gaze roamed over her.

"No problem. I've waited fifteen years for Olivia Miles to come back to Friday Harbor. I'm going to soak up every opportunity I can to hang out with you." The serious delivery of his words had her mouth slightly dropping open as he flashed a pleased grin. "Rest," he reiterated as he stepped outside and hunkered under his rain jacket against the crisp breeze. She shut the door, the glass rattling as a gust of wind decided to assault the boardwalk outside. A dreary day was turning out to be a blessing as she yawned into her hand. A bright beam of sunlight filtered through the door, landing on the honey wooden floors and had her bending forward to peer under the store's outside awning to peer at the sky. Amidst the heavy-laden clouds, the radiant sun waited patiently to burst forth, its rays finding whatever available crack in the clouds they could to shine down on Friday Harbor. Then the clouds shifted and the sunbeam disappeared, leaving a gloominess to the store. She spotted Matt's blue jacket as he stopped briefly to speak with the same fisherman she'd seen him talking to yesterday. *Perhaps that is Handy*, she thought, but she hadn't realized she was staring until the stranger raised his hand her direction and waved at her. Matt turned, and his eyes settled on the storefront. She saw his white teeth as his lopsided smile spread across his face. He gave one last wave as he and the man headed further up the walk towards the pier. *How embarrassing*, she reproached herself for staring after him. She quickly backed away from the front windows and back towards the register. Today would be a good day to look over the store's sales records. If she was aiming to break Bilbo and Mamie's records, she needed to know her baseline. And perhaps, the numbers would take her mind off Matthew... "Matt," she corrected herself in a scolding whisper. "He goes by Matt."

~

The currents and eddies had pushed him out to the west side of the islands and up the Frazier River for most of the afternoon, which wasn't terrible considering the cloud-covered sky. The sun peeked through just enough to keep the chill away while the clouds provided much needed protection from its harsh rays. But he did smell. Boy, did he smell. He held the front of his shirt to his nose and gagged. Herring guts lingered and he blamed Handy for the stench. Preparing bait buckets was not exactly what Matt had in mind when he offered to help. But despite the horrendous smell, he loved the work— missed it some days— and Handy was kind enough to let him join in on the crews whenever he could.

He walked towards his house boat, his ongoing remodel project that floated alongside a handful of others along the back-end pier. He'd shower and change and then pick up Olivia. When the water steamed, he ducked his head and let it seep through his hair. Eyes on the drain, he saw dirt and grime circle and disappear along with the weariness he'd begun to feel. He was tired. Not mentally, but physically, and he was glad Olivia had decided against continuing her store overhaul project for tonight, because he knew he'd have volunteered to help again. And if he were honest, he just didn't have it in him for tonight. The idea of sitting at Ramsey's and drinking a cold one sounded much more appealing than rearranging Anchors Aweigh. And enjoying Olivia's company... well, that always sounded good to him. The more he was around her, the more he liked. Which then in turn made him want to be around her even more. Not a bad conundrum in his book.

Shutting off the water, he stepped out and made quick work of shaving his five o clock shadow before dressing in the last clean shirt he owned, a simple grey t-shirt that he wore with the same jeans he had worn the day before— the only pair not covered in fish guts at the moment. Wasn't his best effort in dressing to impress a woman, but it was him and the best he could do for now. Besides, it was Ramsey's. Normally, Matt would just show up covered in fish guts and not care, but there was Olivia to think about this time. He didn't think she'd appreciate his lingering stench over the course of the evening.

He flicked his lights off and locked the door, a new habit he still wasn't used to. But ever since the Smith boys raided a few houseboats several months ago, Matt didn't want to risk his home to unwanted guests. He pocketed his keys as he walked up the boardwalk towards Anchors Aweigh. He'd barely lifted his hand to knock when the door swung open. Olivia stepped out in a rush. "Hey." Her voice was winded as she immediately turned to lock the door behind her. He brushed his eyes over her and liked the little black dress she'd chosen. It was a bit upscale for Ramsey's, but she looked stunning, and he found he liked the way it accentuated her slim shoulders and long neck. Her soft hair was brushed into a messy twist at the nape of her neck and loose tendrils fell, framing her face. Effortless was the first word that came to mind. Women of all ages might stand before the mirror for hours to try and achieve the same look, but for Liv, that level of beauty was just effortless. She was just naturally stunning. "Matt?" she asked, waving a hand in front of his face.

He flinched and mustered a smile. "Sorry, I was distracted by how beautiful you look."

She playfully rolled her eyes as she dropped her keys into her clutch. "Riiiight."

"Seriously," Matt paused, gently resting his hand on her arm. "You look really... nice, Liv."

"Well, thanks." She waited for him to start walking and followed his directions. "I wasn't sure what to wear tonight, not having ever been. Is this okay? I have something nicer if need be."

"Oh no, you're fine. Dressed better than anyone else that will be there, I'm sure."

"So, am I overdressed? Should I change?" Doubt clouded her features and he grinned.

"You might be a tad overdressed, but— no, no, no, no you don't." He turned a fleeing Olivia's shoulders back in the direction of Ramsey's. "You look gorgeous and I am not going to be responsible for all the fellas missing out on seeing such a beautiful woman."

Olivia blushed and then stopped. "Now I'm nervous."

Laughing, he pulled her into his side and wrapped his arm around her shoulders. He felt her drape her arm around his waist and they walked companionably down the side street towards the bar. "Don't be nervous. It's just a bunch of locals relaxing after a long week. Nothing to be nervous about."

"Alright."

"Besides, everyone here loves Bilbo and Mamie, so you have automatic points in your favor."

"That's good to know." He felt some of the tension flee from her shoulders, but he didn't remove his arm and she didn't step out of his hold. They walked up to the old metal building, where the old fishing nets draped on a hook by the door, the empty buckets turned upside down for added seating when some of the men needed to step outside for a smoke, and the lingering smell of fish and sea welcomed them to Ramsey's. Matt shoved open the heavy wooden door, the carvings on the outside displaying what others called the Tale of Moby Dick, but Ramsey called his self-portrait. A man, complete with bulging arm muscles, battling tumultuous seas and a giant fish found his home in the deeply engraved surface.

"This is it. Just a rusty hole in the wall, I'm afraid. But I hope you have a good time."

"It is not down on any map. True places never are," Olivia said quietly.

"Moby Dick." Matt chuckled and pointed at the carving on the door.

"That's what it made me think of."

"It does everyone else as well, minus Ramsey. Don't even get him started on the image." They stepped inside to chatter and music and the smell of grease as bar snacks were being handed out to various patrons at barreled tables cluttered with sauces and beer bottles. "Do you quote books often?" he asked.

Olivia chuckled. "Not really. I'm just particularly fond of that story because Bilbo read it to me years ago. And he'd read me bits and pieces when I came to Friday Harbor. Do you? You seemed to know immediately what I was referencing."

"I wish I could say yes, but the truth is that's one of the few." He felt her stiffen beside him and he noticed everyone in the room stared at them. "Don't be nervous," he whispered as he led her towards the bar.

Ramsey, a robust man in his mid-forties boasting a scraggily beard of deep auburn that matched what little hair graced his head, greeted them with sparkling blue eyes that held the secrets of his jolly temperament in their assessment of Olivia.

"A guest." Ramsey grinned, showcasing a chipped center tooth in the top row. "What will it be, sweetheart?"

Olivia slid onto a vacant stool, Matthew slipping next to her as he stood in between her and the occupied stool next to her. "White wine, please."

Ramsey nodded and reached under the counter, popping the top on a light beer, he slid it across the counter. Without complaint, Olivia lifted it to her lips and took a long sip. She released a contented sigh. "My favorite."

Ramsey guffawed and winked at her. "I like your style, little one. What's your name?"

"Olivia. Olivia Miles."

"Ah. *Olivia*." He eyed Matthew next to her and his eyebrows danced. "Well, you need to sock that boy in the face." He pointed to Matt. "Because he's been spreading boldfaced lies about you."

Olivia's brows rose in surprise as she turned to face Matthew. He held up his hands in innocence, shooting a warning glance towards Ramsey.

Ramsey's shoulders shook as he bit back a laugh. "He said you were pretty, but he didn't say you were the prettiest girl I'd ever lay eyes on."

Olivia smirked as she took another sip of her beer. "I've got my eye on you." She squinted towards Ramsey. "You're trouble."

Ramsey chortled and winked at her as he handed Matt his own beer. "I like her, Summers. You two grab a table, I'll tell Sid you're here."

Matt guided Olivia to one of the barrels.

"Who is Sid?" Olivia asked.

"The cook." Matthew leaned back in his chair, the first time of the day he'd fully relaxed. "I tend to gorge myself on cheese sticks when I come. Did I not tell you that?"

She laughed. "No, but I like your style. I could easily go for some greasy cheese sticks."

"Then you're in luck. No better grease in the harbor than Ramsey's." He toasted towards her.

Her smile waned a touch as she leaned forward to lower her level of conversation. "Thank you for bringing me out tonight. I know it's not how you probably imagined unwinding on your Friday night, but... I appreciate you showing me a local spot."

"You act as if I'm doing you a favor." Matt shook his head. "I wanted to hang out with you tonight, Liv. If it hadn't been here at Ramsey's, I would have chosen somewhere else."

"Oh, well I didn't mean I—" Her response was drowned out by the arrival of Jake and several other men as they came through the door in a burst of cheers and howls, a stringer of fish in their hands. Jake spotted Olivia and headed their direction, his bright smile hidden beneath a muddy face. He reeked of mud bottoms and fish, and Matt watched as Olivia discretely held her breath at his arrival.

"Whoa, pungent much?" Matt waved his hand in front of his face as Jake laughed.

"Best catch of the day after you wimped out on us."

"Ha. Right." Matt rolled his eyes as Jake squatted beside the table to be on eye level with Olivia.

"I see why you bailed though... guess you had to get all gussied up for the lady." He grinned at Olivia. "Good to see you, Olivia. Give me a few and

I'll join you guys." He walked away and Olivia turned wide eyes towards Matt.

"Please tell me he means to take a shower."

Matt laughed as he shook his head. "Probably not."

"Matthew, he... he smells terrible. How are we supposed to eat?"

Matt threw his head back as he laughed, and he couldn't contain it even if he tried when she tried to shush him. "Oh Olivia, you're too funny. Most of the people in here are like Jake. I am honestly only showered because I knew I would be meeting up with you. Otherwise, I wouldn't have bothered either."

Annoyance marred her brow. "Well, I don't want them to think I made you clean up or that you had to look presentable on my behalf." She flicked her hand at his shirt and pants.

"They don't think that," he assured her. "They just understand why I did."

"And why's that?" she asked.

"Obviously to impress you." He could tell his honesty surprised her by the rise of color to her cheeks.

"And why would you want to do that?"

"For one thing, I didn't want to scare you off with foul odors, and second, I know we have fond memories of one another, but the last thing I want to do is taint our new memories with fish guts."

Her nose curled at his term and he grinned.

"We're old friends. You have no need to impress me, Matthew. I like you the way you are."

"And I'm glad. But sometimes, it's nice to have a shower and escort a beautiful woman along the boardwalk without feeling self-conscious."

"Who's self-conscious?" Jake asked as he pulled the nearest chair towards their table and sat.

"Certainly not you," Matt told him and scrunched his nose.

Ramsey slid two baskets of hot cheese sticks on the table and Jake, with freshly scrubbed hands, reached in and helped himself. He bit off half a stick and held his mouth open a moment. "Hawt." He tried to huff a bit and Matt just shook his head at his friend. Olivia bit back a smile. "So, Olivia," Jake rested his elbows on the table as he grabbed Matt's beer and finished it. "You tired of this guy yet?" He thumbed towards Matt. "Because if you are, I was going to see if you wanted to go out on the boat tomorrow. I've got this nice little—"

"I'm taking her on a tour," Matt interrupted.

Jake's invite trailed off. "A tour?" His attention turned back to Olivia. "Seriously, I can give you a way better tour on my boat. Plus, it's not full of annoying tourists. What do you say?" He flashed his charming smile once again and Matt just knew Olivia would cave, as most women did, to the charms of Jake.

"Actually, I'm looking forward to the tour. I haven't been on one since I was young. It will be nice to witness the orcas as an adult. Besides... Matt's promised to let me steer the boat."

"Oh, did he?" Jake turned towards his friend in shock and Matt laughed, lightly tugging one of Olivia's stray tendrils.

"Not quite, but I guess that can be arranged." He beamed as she gave a little victory punch in the air and cheered. Jake gave her a high five.

"Nicely done," Jake complimented. "This guy is a bit of a stickler when it comes to *The Voyager*. He must really like you to let you get behind the wheel. I've been asking him for years."

"It's because I'm cooler than you," Olivia baited, surprising both men.

"Oh, now I see how it's going to be." Jake tossed his half-eaten cheese stick into the basket and pretended to dust his fingers. "Shall we duel?"

Olivia leaned forward, challenge in her eyes, and Matt's heart skipped a beat at the sight. "Name your terms, fisherman."

"Ooooh, I like her." Jake punched Matt's shoulder. "How are you at Poker?"

"Fair." She shrugged her shoulders.

"Dominoes?" She mimicked her previous pose.

"Which do you prefer?"

"I try all things; achieve what I can."

Matthew burst into laughter at her quote from Moby Dick. "Nicely done." He reached for her hand and kissed the back of it as he patted Jake on the shoulder. "I think it should be a battle of wits, for Olivia has already climbed ahead."

"I'm lost."

"I know," Matt reiterated.

"Is this some sort of inside joke?"

Olivia and Matt grinned at one another as Ramsey stepped forward, sliding fresh beers in front of all of them and collecting the empty bottles.

"Ramsey, I think we have trouble here." Jake pointed at the two across from him and Ramsey nodded.

"I like trouble." Ramsey winked at Olivia and she returned it with a smirk.

Jake relaxed in his chair, sipping on his beer. "So, Olivia," he continued. "You like being back so far?"

"I do. It's different, but in a good way."

"How's it different?" Jake asked.

"Well, for one, it's not as big as I remember it. I remember the boardwalk seemed huge, but it's just about a street's width. The boats seemed enormous, and they're just small houseboats and sail boats. Little things like that."

"And the people?" Jake asked, nodding towards Matthew.

"Grown." She shared another smile with Matt.

"Yeah, crazy you two go way back. I remember Matthew in those days. I remember him being so hung up on you too."

Matt choked on his sip and had Jake leaning forward and offering a friendly pat on his back. "Easy, tiger. I'm not going to tell your secrets."

Olivia's brow rose at that, but she didn't push. Thankfully.

"What was your favorite thing to do here when you were younger?" Jake asked.

"That's a long list." Olivia took a bite of a cheese stick as she mulled over his question. "Obviously seeing Bilbo and Mamie. Time with them was never wasted." Wistfulness captured her tone as her eyes stared off a moment. "Swimming, fishing, sailing." She looked to Matt then and a tenderness swelled behind her eyes. "Time with this guy." She squeezed his hand. "We had some crazy adventures, didn't we?"

Matt nodded, linking his fingers with hers and liking that she didn't remove them as she continued. "Remember that time we stole Mr. Scheuster's bucket of oysters?" She giggled as Jake's eyes widened.

"And you lived to tell the tale?" he asked.

Nodding, she pointed to Matt. "This guy jumped the seawall, leaving me standing in the middle of the street, bucket in hand."

"Not a very good thief then?" Jake laughed.

"Oh, I didn't get caught. Matthew just *thought* it was old man Scheuster who was about to walk out of the bait shop. Only it wasn't." She nudged Matt playfully in the arm. "Scaredy-cat hopped the wall and, *SPLASH*, into the ocean he went for absolutely *no* reason."

Jake laughed along with her at young Matt's cowardice.

"To be fair, I was skating on thin ice with Mr. Scheuster already," Matt defended. "If he had caught me, I'd have been banned for life from his shop. And since he was the only bait shop in town at the time, I needed him."

"So, what happened to the bucket of oysters?" Jake asked.

"I ate them," Olivia admitted. "Every last one. By myself."

"You didn't even meet up with her after that?" Jake asked Matt.

Matt leaned back in his chair and crossed his arms over his chest, his right boot propped against the table to stabilize the tilt of his chair. "I did meet up with her, she just wouldn't share."

Jake reached forward and gave Olivia a fist bump.

"Winner takes it all," she said with a small shrug. "I walked across the entire boardwalk carrying the contraband while Matthew was swimming with the porpoises." She and Jake shared another laugh at his expense, and Matt just rolled his eyes.

"I was not swimming with the porpoises." Even to his ears, his rebuttal was weak.

"I would never have abandoned you," Jake bragged. "Mr. Scheuster and I had an understanding back then."

"Oh?"

"Yeah, he knew I would always buy bait for the tourists at the resort, so he pretty much let me help myself to whatever I wanted."

"If I'd only met you then," Olivia teased.

Matt saw the intrigue spark in Jake's eyes and knew his friend was interested in Olivia. True to Jake form, he leaned forward, his elbows resting on the table as he leaned towards Olivia in conversation. He flashed the perfectly straight smile, complete with dimples, that always charmed the ladies, and he made sure Olivia had his full attention. Matt slowly began to feel like an intruder. Until he felt her blue eyes glance his way. She stood to her feet and both men shifted in their seats to stand. She waved them down.

"Don't get up. I'll be back in a few minutes." She patted Matt's shoulder as she walked towards the restroom.

"She is fantastic." Jake popped another cheese stick in his mouth. "If she was half as great then as she is now, I can see why you were so hung up on her."

"Yeah, she's pretty great."

"So, have you guys rekindled the old flame yet?" Jake asked, rubbing his hands together as if starting a fire.

"That would be a no." Matt shook his head.

"Do you want to?"

Matt sighed. "She's only here for the summer. What would be the point?"

"So, she's fair game?" Jake asked.

Matt's entire body stiffened. "She's not *game* at all."

"Whoa, whoa, whoa," Jake held up his hands to ward off Matt's temper. "I was just asking if you had plans with her. I like her. She's beautiful. Funny. I'd like to get to know her better while she's here. I'm just making sure I don't have anyone standing in my way."

His way? Matt scoffed. As much as he loved his friend, Jake's assumption that he could just swoop in and steal Olivia set Matt's blood to boiling. "Not sure if she's interested in a summer fling, Jake."

His friend shrugged as he continued to eat. "Guess she can be the judge of that." He wriggled his eyebrows as Olivia came back to the table.

"So, what'd I miss?" she asked.

"Nothing." Matt forced a smile her way as he watched Jake scoot his chair closer to her and begin boasting of his successful fishing day, making sure to point out every flaw in Matt's own work. Matt took a long sip of his drink. It was going to be a long evening.

« CHAPTER FIVE »

Olivia wasn't quite sure how much longer she could stand stories from Jake. Though he was friendly, she had hoped to spend more time in conversation with Matt versus his friend. But Matt sat coolly to the side, and other than a few stiff smiles, he'd barely spoken a word. Not that he could fit one in if he wanted to due to Jake's chatty behavior. When Ramsey walked up with the two styrofoam containers she'd ordered on her way to the restroom, she was relieved to rise to her feet.

"Thank you for this."

"My pleasure. You come see us anytime now. You're a local, and you're always welcome."

Touched at his offer, Olivia gave him a friendly hug. The big man awkwardly patted her back as he wasn't used to such interaction. "Thank you," she repeated. She looked to Jake and Matt. "I'm going to head back to the shop. I'm pretty beat." She saw Jake begin rising to his feet and inwardly cringed at the thought of him offering to walk her back and having to listen to him drone on and on about himself even more. She looked to Matt. "Walk me back?" she asked.

Matt's brows rose in surprise, but he nodded and stood, tossing several bills onto the table.

"Jake, it was fun." She patted his shoulder in passing as she lifted her containers from the table. "I look forward to seeing you around."

"Likewise. And hey, maybe once you're settled in a bit more, you'll let me whisk you away on a real sailboat," he teased, looking at Matt in challenge and then back to Olivia.

"Maybe so." She smiled as they walked towards the door. When they stepped outside, the fresh air and light breeze was a welcome reprieve. She inhaled a deep breath and sighed. "Finally." She cast an amused smirk towards Matt.

"Did you not enjoy Ramsey's?" he asked, concern washing over his face.

"It was fun. I was just about to pass out if I had to smell Jake any longer."

His lips twitched, and the one corner that always tilted a hint higher than the other, slowly crept upward.

She pointed towards the seawall, which wasn't exactly a seawall but more of a ledge that separated the boardwalk from the rows and rows of houseboats that tied off along the pier. "Walk for a bit?"

"Sure." Matt shoved his hands in his pockets and let her lead the way.

"You've been quiet," she pointed out. "Did I upset you in some way?"

Matt shook his head. "No. Absolutely not."

"Oh. Well, you seemed... aggravated a bit. I wasn't sure if I'd done something to annoy you."

Again, he shook his head, but he offered no explanation for his moody behavior. She watched as the breeze danced its way through his thick hair. She held up her containers. "Want some cheese sticks?"

"You ordered more?" he asked.

She grimaced. "I couldn't eat with... well, that smell."

His handsome face finally split into his usual smile before he laughed. "That bad, huh?"

"Bleh! How could you not smell him? It was awful. The last thing I wanted to do was eat. I feel like I can even taste the smell now if I think about it too much."

"Then it's best not to think about it." Matt popped the lid of one of the containers and handed her a cheese stick. He retrieved one as well and bit off the end.

Olivia climbed onto the ledge of the seawall and sat, dangling her legs over the water. Matt did the same as they watched the lights of Friday Harbor and the houseboats illuminate the night.

"I forgot how quiet it is here." Olivia looked up at the star-filled sky and closed her eyes. "I hear the waves. Not the white-caps, but the soft and lazy aftereffects that jostle the boat beneath your feet. I hear the quiet hum of voices, probably from a television on one of the boats, but it's comforting. I also hear giggles, though I know they aren't real, but just a memory I have of running up and down the docks with you all those years ago." She opened her eyes and turned to find him staring at her. "Is it weird?" she asked. "That I can remember every single moment from that summer even after all this time? That through the years whenever I would get overwhelmed or even heartbroken, I'd think back to that summer and it would instantly calm me. Encourage me. Make me smile."

"It's not weird at all." Matt's deep voice contrasted with the soft sounds of the night, but she liked the tone of it. And much like the other sounds and feelings surrounding her, it comforted. "I've thought about that summer a lot over the years as well. I'm glad it was as important to you as it was to me."

"I would have come back in a heartbeat." Her tone, laced with urgency, had her turning to face him. "I want you to know that. And I know it was a long time ago and we're adults now and it probably doesn't even matter, but I want you to know that. That if I could have chosen my own path, I would have come right back here. To you." A sad smile crossed her face as she turned back to face the water. "I loved that summer." Her voice carried on the breeze as her hair began to slip from its clips and tickle her face and neck. She felt Matt's fingers lightly brush her cheek as he tucked wayward strands behind her ear. Turning, she found him studying her. "Tell me what you're thinking now," she pressed, hoping he'd take a turn and bask in the old, yet familiar banter they'd used on the back of his sailboat each time they'd sneak away for some ocean adventures.

He closed his eyes and faced the breeze and it was her turn to study him. She liked being able to peruse his face without worrying about staring too long. He'd matured into a handsome man. The sun had kept his skin a healthy tan, but the effects of its rays had left small wrinkles at the corners of his eyes. From squinting or smiling, she didn't know, but she'd bet on the latter. His nose was straight, minus the small hump in the center that was the result of them running through the docks and his misjudgment of an untethered boom that disrupted his path. She liked that the mark of that great chase was one he carried with him. He'd been chasing her at the time, and both had been clumsy and foolish to run through the crowded docks. "I hear boats moving through the water," he began, his voice interrupting her trip down memory lane. "I hear you, crunching on a cheese stick." He peeked through one eye at her and she shoved his shoulder. Chuckling, he closed his eye and faced the ocean once more. "I hear the rush of footsteps, the excited squeals of kids and adults alike as they hurry about the boardwalk." The game was to share two current sounds or feelings before sharing a memory. She listened, curious as to what memory he would choose to share. "I hear your mom yelling for you and me begging you not to go. I remember watching you leave and Bilbo coming up behind me, resting his hand on my shoulder. "She'll be back one of these days, kiddo. Keep your head up." He mimicked Bilbo's deep baritone and had her smiling. He opened his eyes and looked at her. "I wasn't the only one sad to see you leave."

"I know. I started calling Bilbo and Mamie the Sunday after I left and never stopped. It then became a routine. One we keep, even to this day."

"So, I take it you will be hearing from them this weekend?"

"I'm sure of it." Tenderness swelled in her heart.

They sat in silence a moment, both enraptured by the sounds of the waves. "Remember that time you dared me to walk up and down the seawall?" she asked.

"How could I forget? You lasted like ten steps."

"They were slippery," she defended. "And I sprained my ankle, thank you very much."

"Because when you slipped you decided to fall towards the boardwalk and not the water," Matt teased.

"Rookie mistake." Grinning, she stood to her feet and slipped off her sandals.

"What are you doing?"

"I'm going to redeem myself." She climbed onto the ledge. "It certainly doesn't seem as far down as I remember... easy peasy."

Matt moved their food cartons to give her access to the small stretch of concrete. The narrow ledge was cold beneath her feet. "If you fall, fall that way," he suggested, pointing towards the water.

She rolled her eyes, exaggerating her annoyance by moaning heavenward. Her right foot slipped, and she hurriedly rebalanced her feet. Matthew was right beside her, his hand on her arm to prevent her from diving into the water. "Easy now." He chuckled.

"Don't distract me and I won't fall."

"I'm helping you." He released her arm and walked beside her as she moved slowly down one ledge to the next, the stair-step of the boardwalk's wall growing grimier the lower she walked. The water lapped beneath her, the cold splatter landing on her exposed feet was cold and yet, still tempting. She continued her path and a door swung open on one of the houseboats with a loud bang. She gasped, her left foot slipping and dipping into the water. She teetered, her arms waving to catch herself, and she felt herself falling towards the cold depths. Squealing, she felt Matt's arms come around her and swing her back onto the dock landing. She gripped his arms as her heart hammered in her chest. "That was a close one." Her head fell just beneath his chin and she basked in the luxury of his closeness and rested her forehead against his chest. *Odd*, she thought, *that after all these years, he still smelled the same.* Ocean and sun.

She pulled back a step, his arms still around her waist as she looked up at him. "Good catch."

"I was prepared."

"Hey, Matt!" The man that'd stepped out of his boat hailed from down the dock. Matt turned his head. "When ya' get a minute, I think we're having trouble with the antenna!" The man shuffled back inside his house, his door clapping closed behind him.

"Is it past your curfew?" Olivia jested.

"Funny." He tugged on her hair and released her. Immediately missing his warmth and the tenderness of the moment, she regretfully slipped her sandals back onto her feet.

"That's my neighbor and he refuses to invest in cable, so he props up a series of antennas and foil to achieve the best signal for his nightly television binge. Some of those antennas and foil bridges have slinked their way onto my boathouse as well. Apparently, I have better signal than he does."

Olivia laughed. "I see. Well, I'd hate to interrupt his programming."

Matt pulled her to him and draped his arm over her shoulders as he led her up the boardwalk. "He can wait. I mean to finish my night by escorting you back safely to your home... like a true gentleman."

"Well, that's nice of you." She grinned up at him and thought she caught his gaze wandering to her lips, but when they passed under a lamp post, he'd redirected his gaze towards their path. She was surprised to find herself disappointed, though she knew her line of thinking was out of bounds. She'd just come back. She barely knew Matthew, and yet, here she was hoping he'd *kiss* her? She mentally shook away the thought. She was only here for the summer. She was only here to run the store. She was only here temporarily. *Yes, that's what she'd keep telling herself.* She'd left Matthew behind all those years ago. Life had kept them apart. It was meant to be that way. He was her friend of Friday Harbor. Nothing more.

Or, she told herself, *perhaps he could be more.* Should be more. *Would* be more if she'd let her guard down. But deep down she knew that wouldn't be fair to either of them. Because come September, she'd be gone again. And as hard as it was to leave Matthew Summers fifteen years ago, she imagined it would be twice as hard now. She let him hover as she unlocked the door to Anchors Aweigh and then she thanked him once again for the fun night. They had that awkward moment of whether to hug, shake hands, or even kiss, the thought giving her butterflies as he opted for a hug and kissed her cheek. She was still pressing her fingers to the spot when she watched him walk back towards the docks, his familiar strut with hands in his pockets and no hurry in his steps etching itself into her memory.

~

"All aboard." Matt extended his hand and helped Olivia onto *The Voyager*. His mother stood on the docks and waved. She held her hand up to her lips. "Don't you worry about the store, Olivia.

It's in good hands." She wiggled her fingers and then watched as her son escorted Olivia up the steps towards the wheel. "She's a bit excited to be at the store today." He opened the door to the captain's cabin. "Thanks for agreeing to let her help out."

"She's helping *me*," Olivia corrected. "I wouldn't be able to come if she didn't help, so it's I who am in her debt." She looked down as he placed a bulky handheld radio in her palm. "A walkie-talkie?"

"We prefer the term radio," he laughed, as she turned it on and a voice barked through the line. "That's Larry."

"Why do I need this?" she asked.

"Well, co-captain, I figure if you are to ride in the cabin long enough you might get bored. So, if you venture down on the decks, I have a way of reaching out to you."

"Smart thinking." She beamed up at him and their eyes held a moment.

He saw the excitement in her blue gaze and was glad he helped put it there. Larry's voice boomed through the radio and had Matt taking a step towards the wheel, grabbing his own radio to respond. "Anchors Aweigh." He flipped a few switches, pulled a couple of levers, and slowly the boat shifted and began drifting away from the dock. Olivia gripped the back of the swivel chair that stood behind him and he motioned for her to step towards him.

"I need to find my sea legs, first. It's been awhile."

"Roger that." Matt expertly weaved his way out of the harbor and out towards open waters. He reached forward and tapped a red button. "Good morning, folks, this is Captain Matt. Welcome aboard *The Voyager*. We are glad you're here and hope to show you the best that the San Juan Islands have to offer. It is also your lucky day, for we have a co-captain aboard for this morning's cruise. Captain Olivia is aboard. If you see her around, give her an 'All hail the captain'." He turned and grinned at her as she rolled her eyes. He tossed her a captain's hat and she placed it on her head. Shooting her a thumbs up, he went back to his introductory speech over safety rules and regulations, the schedule and locations they were headed and what to expect. "There are over 30 species in the oceanic dolphin family, and you'll be surprised to know that orcas are part of this particular family even though most people consider them in the whale family," he continued. "They can also be found in all of the world's oceans. They get around," he chuckled as he winked at Olivia. "They're social creatures and you will rarely see an orca by his lonesome. In fact, what we will be aiming for today is an entire pod for you guys. Besides orcas, I'll be sure to point out any other friends we find along the way. Typically, this includes our buddies the Dall porpoises. They like to ride the waves, so to speak, and they are particularly fond of *The Voyager*. Not to brag, but I think they have good taste."

He paused a moment as he began turning the wheel to gradually shift another direction. "Harbor seals are also pretty common, so keep your eye out for their heads poking up through the waters. Now—" He paused for dramatic effect. "One of the most mysterious, yet numerous whales in the world, the minke whale, may grace us with his presence. What makes them a hard to spot is that they can hold their breath for long periods of time. Up to 20 minutes." Matt glanced over his shoulder at Olivia and saw she was staring out over the water contentedly listening. "So, they come up for a bit of air and quickly disappear into the depths once again. So, keep an eye out. Maybe you're the lucky bunch who will see one. And off we go." He turned off the intercom and then turned to Olivia. "Got your sea legs yet?"

She walked towards him and he motioned towards the wheel. "What?" she asked.

"Take it," he ordered.

Eyes wide, Olivia shook her head. "I can't drive this thing."

Laughing, he grabbed her hand and pulled her towards him and the wheel. "First off, it's steer, not drive. Second," He placed her hands on two handles and covered them with his own. "It's not hard. We have a northwest bearing, so just keep it steady. Besides, you told Jake you'd take the wheel. We'd hate to disappoint him." He plopped an extra captain's hat on his head, released her hands, and sat in the chair as she gripped the wheel, knuckles white. "Relax, Liv, and take a breath." He slowly saw her shoulders relax.

"Like I care what Jake thinks," Olivia muttered. Matt choked back a snicker as he thought of Jake's disappointed expression if he had heard her quick dismissal of him.

The radio crackled to life and an unknown voice flooded the cabin. "Porpoises on starboard."

Matt hopped to his feet and tapped the intercom. "Well, folks, it looks like we have some visitors. If you are on the starboard side, you should see some of our friendly pals the Dall porpoises. Now, you port side people don't worry and don't hurry over to the other side, we don't want to tip." He saw Liv's worried expression and laughed. "Kidding. We won't tip. Just keep your heads and know that this is just the beginning of the tour. We have a ways to go and will see much more." He turned off the intercom and went back to studying the waters. He reached over and gently rested a hand on one of the wheel handles and altered their path to keep their bearing. "Doing good, Liv." He saw her confidence bloom as she became more comfortable behind the wheel. She looked cute wearing his hat and she seemed completely in tune with her surroundings. She gasped and pointed towards the horizon. "Is that what I think it is?"

Matt picked up a pair of binoculars, his mouth serious as he waited for some sort of movement or sign the orcas were close. "It's a bit early for us to see them. I don't see anything."

Disappointment sagged her shoulders momentarily and then her face brightened. "There." She pointed again and he turned back and raised the binoculars once again. He lowered them and looked at her. "I don't see anything, Liv."

She pointed. "Look, look, look. You're missing it." She nudged his hands up towards his face as he gripped the binoculars.

He quickly raised them to his face and sighed. "Liv—"

"Don't even turn to look at me, keep staring at the horizon. I could have sworn I saw—"

He saw sprays of water lift above the sea-line and Liv cheered. "Tell me you saw that."

"I see it." He smirked. "Nice job, Captain." He took the wheel from her and grabbed the radio to ready his crew for an orca sighting. "You head down to the first level, starboard side. You'll get the best view from there."

Without hesitation, she darted towards the cabin doors, her excitement bubbling forth as she halted her steps and flashed him one last smile. A smile, he remembered, that used to affect him exactly the same way it did now. He saw his captain's hat bop down the steps and then readied himself to flip the intercom button. He wanted to make sure Olivia settled in down below before he announced the sighting. He wanted to make sure she received the best position possible. When he felt ample time had passed, he pressed the red button.

~

"Spotted by our lovely Captain Olivia, you guys are in for a real treat. The orcas have decided to show up early for us." Matt's voice boomed over the speakers and excited chatter spread through the crowd. "We'll approach the orcas and starboard side will see first sighting. We will then circle round for the port side to have a viewing as well. Good sighting, Captain Olivia." He clicked off and Olivia found herself just as excited as his passengers. She leaned against the railing and felt others crowding around her, along with voices of "There's Captain Olivia, stand by her! She knows what to look for!" She wanted to laugh at that but posed for several photos as people wished to have a photo with her just as much as with the orcas appearing in the background. Matt was going to hear about her stardom, that was for certain. She lifted her face to the wind and felt the light touches of sea spray *The Voyager* tossed in her wake. That smell of seawater and sunshine seeped into her soul and unaware of their power, she felt her feet hit the bottom rail as she climbed. Holding onto Matt's hat, she leaned out over the side as far as she could to see the pod in its entirety. Families crushed together, the little ones closest to the action to witness the enormity of the ocean creatures. When the first orca rose from the water, a chorus of oohs and aahs drifted around the decks. Olivia marveled at the sight of the smooth black and white beasts that emerged, shooting spray above the surface. The slap of the tails on the water had the crowd squealing with delight, all ages admiring God's creation of such creatures. Her attention was thwarted as she heard her name. Reaching for the radio clipped to her pants, she raised the walkie to her lips. "This is Olivia."

"Captain." Matt's voice made her grin.

"Aye, this be yer captain speaking." She mimicked the best pirate impersonation she could muster as she waited to hear what he wished to tell her.

She heard his laugh before he began talking. "We're about to circle around for portside viewing. Mind heading that direction?"

"Not at all. Headed that way." She ducked her head to avoid being snapped in a family photo as she maneuvered through the crowd and towards the opposite side of the ship. She noticed several excited faces as she emerged near the railing of portside and as *The Voyager* began to make its turn, the excitement turned to glee as other viewers realized it was finally their turn to see the orcas.

Olivia grinned when she spotted a handful of porpoises adjusting their course as Matt steered a small half circle and made the turn. The porpoises glided along and leapt a few happy splashes in the wake of the waves as cameras snapped and children cheered. But they were just a small taste of what the kids would see, and Olivia watched one small boy in particular to see his face light up when he caught his first glance at an orca. Matt's voice carried over the speaker as he announced the sighting to the port side, and the little boy's eyes widened in astonishment. His father lifted him up and cradled him in the crook of his elbow as he pointed to the spray spewing up from below. A shift in the wind had Olivia flashing her gaze towards the orcas as well, as if she could sense the upcoming act. Seconds later, a black and white streak emerged and jumped, soaring through the air. For mere seconds, no one blinked for fear they'd miss the remarkable sight. In awe, Matt's audience grew silent as another emerged and then another. The ongoing cycle of oceanic beauty had Olivia leaning against the railing smiling. She remembered the first time she witnessed the orcas, and it awed her in equal measure in the present as it had back then. She snuck her way towards the stairwell, only being captured twice for photos and made her way towards Matt. She'd seen the orcas down below, now she wanted to see them from his vantage point. When she opened the door, he turned, his lean face splitting into that familiar grin that suddenly made her heart drop clear to her toes. He looked completely at ease behind the wheel, relaxed, and exquisitely happy with himself and what he was doing. She'd never witnessed anyone seeming so natural and content with their profession and life. She also hadn't realized how much she'd *missed* him.

Oh, she knew she'd missed him. For the first year or two after she left, she'd missed him terribly. But standing and watching him now, she realized the depth of that loss. Those years they hadn't kept in touch. What would life be like if they'd continued talking to one another after she left? Would they have kept in touch? Or would their teenage hearts have moved on eventually? She wasn't sure. But, she realized, she sure was glad she was back at Friday Harbor. And as she felt herself float towards him on air crisp with the aroma of ocean, she realized she'd always remember that moment, that flash of him turning around with his unfaltering smile while the sea and horizon shone around him.

« CHAPTER SIX »

"That was a blast." Olivia beamed as she opened the door to Mamie and Bilbo's shop and Matt's mother sat behind the counter lost in one of her romance novels. She rested it on the desk calendar as they entered and smiled in welcome.

"And how was it?" Mrs. Summers asked, already knowing the answer as Olivia tilted her head to look up at her son with bright eyes.

"It was incredible." Olivia linked her arm companionably through Matt's. "Matthew let me steer the ship. I posed for multiple photographs because he somehow convinced the tourists I was a captain of some sort, and the orcas were absolutely stunning. They definitely put on a show for this group." Olivia hurried behind the counter and began sifting through messages stacked by the phone. "How were things here?"

Matt caught the amused expression his mom shot his way as Olivia draped her arm over his mother's shoulders in a brief hug before continuing her duties of checking up on the sales reports. "Why, they were just grand. I've had a steady flow of customers coming in and out. Sold that table and chairs set over there." She pointed towards the front display and Olivia's jaw dropped.

"The whole set?"

"The whole set. They didn't take them with them because I asked if they could pick them up closer to closing time, so you'd be here to fill the space. I figured the window display just wouldn't look right if they were gone, and this happened early in the morning. So, they paid and will be by this afternoon to pick them up."

"You are amazing." Olivia grinned. "Can I keep her?" She looked to Matt for approval and he shrugged his shoulders.

"I don't know... I'm pretty attached to her."

His mother laughed as she waved away their banter. "You two." She shook her head for them to stop, but he could see the faint touches of pink to her cheeks that told him she was pleased with the praise.

"I'm serious, Mrs. Summers," Olivia continued. "If you're interested, I could really use an extra set of hands here and there."

"It's Beth," Matt's mother corrected. "And I would love to help out. Any time."

"How about the rest of the day? Or Monday?"

"I can certainly fill in the rest of the day if you wish to sail out with Matt again."

"Oh, no. I didn't mean that. I actually am working on rearranging the store. I could use someone tending to customers while I shift things around."

Beth looked at her son's disappointed face. "I see. Well, wherever you'd like to use me, I'm yours. I've had more fun chatting with people today. Such a lovely couple came in and—"

Matt tuned his mother out as she and Olivia discussed each sale his mother had made and a potential schedule for her for the following week. Olivia's face was still flushed from walking up the boardwalk and her hair wind-swept from observing the marine life on the tour. Her excitement of seeing the orcas and their impromptu performance animated her movements as she spoke, her hands actively swishing about as she described the sight to his mother. He could tell his mother liked her; the way she acknowledged Olivia with a hand on her arm when they laughed and a nod of approval at Olivia's plans for the store. Olivia stepped around the counter to stand in front of him. "Earth to Matthew." She snapped her fingers in front of his nose and he blinked.

"What?"

"Matthew..." his mother scolded.

"I mean... sorry. I'm sorry. Did I miss something?" He caught his mother's small smirk as she turned back towards a glass globe display and began shifting orbs around on the shelves.

"Your mother asked if I'd like to join you guys for dinner later, and I wasn't sure what time your last tour ended. Does dinner work for you? She wanted us to come out to Lakedale." Olivia waited patiently for his response.

"Lakedale?" he repeated, his mind playing catch up and trying to understand what he'd missed in the conversation.

"Yes, dear. Lakedale. Where your father and I live," Beth called over her shoulder with just enough sarcasm to clear his foggy brain. "You know... the house you grew up in."

"Mom..." He rolled his eyes as he slowly relaxed his shoulders and smiled down at Olivia. He rested his hands on her shoulders. "Sure. Dinner sounds good. I finish at 4, boat cleaned by 5, dinner at 6. That work, Mom?" He glanced over at his mother and she nodded.

"Six would be perfect. I'll have your father fire up the grill." She winked at him before Olivia turned back around and began chatting to her once more.

"We could take the sailboat." He saw Olivia's back straighten at his words. Would she want to be on his sailboat again after all this time? Was she thinking the same thoughts as he was? That the last time they'd sailed together, they had made sweet promises and shared childish declarations of love. Promises that still permeated the air between them, no matter the innocence in which they were delivered. No matter that fifteen years had passed, and fate had brought them together once again. Was it just him?

"We can sail to Lakedale?"

"That would take ages, Matt," his mom interrupted. "Just drive. Otherwise I'd have to pick you two up off Primrose, and you wouldn't be getting home until late... and you know how I feel about you sailing at night. It makes me nervous. Especially with all the dangerous activities happening lately."

"Dangerous activities?" Olivia asked, her eyes imploring for more information.

"Don't freak Liv out, Mom. She means the hooligans that were breaking into some of the houseboats. There hasn't been anything serious. And I've been sailing for almost twenty years, Mom. Even at night."

"Matt—" His mother bit back her request as he sighed.

"I'll drive then."

"You have a car?" Olivia asked in surprise.

Laughing, Matt and Beth nodded. "Of course I do. Why would I not?"

"It's just... you're always on boats. And you live on a boat. I didn't realize..." She flushed.

"Well, you can see it for yourself later this evening. How about that?" he asked.

She nodded bashfully.

"Wonderful." Beth clapped her hands together. "Now, Matt, treat Olivia to some lunch at Leeward's. I'll flip the sign on the door and eat my own lunch. Then you should head back to the docks for your next tour."

"You should come eat with us." Olivia invited.

"I think you two should enjoy each other's company and share highlights from the tour." Beth waved them towards the door. "Plus, I'm at a wonderful spot in my book and *need* to see what happens next."

Matt opened the door for Olivia as she waved goodbye to his mother. As soon as his feet hit the boardwalk, Olivia began gushing about the orcas once more. He draped an arm around her shoulders and pulled her into his side as they walked. She didn't pull away, but instead continued on with enthusiastic hand motions. "Thank you, again, for letting me tag along this morning. It was incredible."

"You're welcome."

"And refreshing. I'd forgotten what a little sea air can do for a person. After working in the store for a few days, it was a nice change of pace."

"I'm glad."

"And I enjoyed seeing you work. Grownup Matt doing his thing." She grinned up at him and he laughed.

"Grownup Matt, huh?"

"I don't know why I was surprised to hear you were still sailing and captaining a cruiser. You loved the water. You loved to sail. But seeing you today..." She paused a moment and they stood outside the door of the restaurant, neither wishing to enter into the noisy atmosphere until she'd finished her thought. "You just fit, Matthew. Here."

She motioned to encompass the entire harbor. "On the water, working with people and boats and old ladies who love you."

He laughed at that and she beamed up at him proudly. "Seriously," She pointed up ahead and saw two ladies from their tour rushing towards them with excited waves. "Your fan club approaches."

He poked her side and she flinched with a giggle as the two elderly ladies swooped in and began recapping the tour and what they enjoyed the most. He patiently listened and watched as Olivia slipped inside without him. He was still caught in conversation when she reappeared ten minutes later with two containers in her hands.

"I hate to steal Captain Matt away from you ladies," Olivia began. "But he's promised me a lunch on the water."

The two women squealed with excitement at the prospect and nudged Olivia towards him, Matt sliding his arm around her waist to navigate her away from the restaurant. Well wishes of a "good lunch," "happy life," and "wonderful time" echoed behind them.

"Thanks for the rescue."

"It's hard being a 'celebrity'."

He playfully shoved her away from him as she giggled.

"They love Captain Matt, who could deny them the chance to speak with you some more?" Olivia asked. "But I'm also hungry, and I know you have to be as well."

"That I am."

"So where should we set up shop?" She held up their food.

"How about this way?" Matt led her down the boardwalk and towards the seawall. They emerged in a small park area and he walked towards a small bench nestled amongst several Jack Pine trees that held sentimental value to the both of them.

Olivia gasped. "No way." She looked up at him in wonder. "I can't believe this is still here." She rushed down the incline towards the bench and ran her hand lovingly over the wooden structure that had definitely seen better days. "Why hasn't anyone torn this down?" she asked.

Matt shrugged. "I may or may not know the owner of this property."

"And who is it?" Olivia asked, settling on the bench with caution. When she saw that it was sturdy, she waved him over.

"Ramsey." Matt accepted his container and popped open the lid.

"And he doesn't mind this awesome display of construction sitting in one of the best spots of his property?"

"No. He doesn't do much with this property. We actually got into a bidding war when it was up for sale. One of the conditions of me backing off and bowing out was that the bench had to stay. He agreed."

Olivia gaped at him. "You tried to buy the property?"

"Years ago. But it wasn't meant to be. However, I do have property closer to Lakedale."

"Remind me to hug Ramsey the next time I see him for keeping this here." She ran her fingers over the carved initials that were engraved on the wood between them as they sat. Her initials and Matthew's. A 'mark of the craftsman,' he'd called it. "Where did we steal this wood from again?"

"My dad's shop," Matt explained. "Jake helped me sneak it onto my sailboat one day. I told him it was a matter of life or death." He laughed as Olivia shook her finger at him.

"Matthew Summers," she scolded.

"It was worth it though, right? We built this spot for us and here we are."

Olivia gazed out at the ocean and noticed the area was well-tended. Flowers planted at the base of trees; the grass neatly mowed. "I don't suppose Ramsey comes out here once a week to maintain it?"

Matt felt his cheeks heat. "I come here quite a bit," he admitted. "It's my thinking spot."

"It's a good spot," Olivia whispered quietly, her mind no doubt wandering to their shared days of building the bench together; the laughter, the bruised thumbs from the hammering, and the secrets shared between them. This was the spot where Olivia had shared about her parents. Little did she know that the fighting and bickering she had lamented in her young assessment would turn out to be the grounds of their divorce just a few months later. Matthew had promised to 'look out for her' and 'be there for her.' But he hadn't.

"Did I upset you by bringing you here?" he asked.

Surprise lit her eyes. "Not at all." She smiled. "I was just thinking about our conversations on this bench."

"Me too."

Understanding fell across her face. "Ah... my parents," she filled in the blanks, and he nodded. "Even then I knew something wasn't right in their marriage. Yes, we had happy moments, but neither of them was truly happy. There was a lot of resentment on my mom's part about my dad's work at the time. My dad disagreed with my mom's ideas for our family... it just wasn't a good mix. Though I never expected my dad to just leave—" she trailed off. "Funny how none of that even seems to matter to me now. It was their lives. I was bitter for a long time about it all. For dragging me away from Friday Harbor. But now... here I am." She shrugged her shoulders. "I could have come back long before now, but I never did. I'm glad Bilbo and Mamie gave me the opportunity. I needed it more than I thought."

She turned her sparkling blue eyes his way and he felt his heart tug towards her. "See... it's a good thinking spot."

Her lips twitched into a contented smile as she leaned over and rested her head against his shoulder. "Tell me what you think about up here."

"Everything. Life. Work. My future. It's always been a good spot. I always remember you when I sit up here. Usually wondering what happened to you, where you ended up."

She rested her chin on his shoulder and faced him. He felt her silent study of his silhouette and turned their noses almost touching. It was odd, the level of comfort they shared with one another after so long an absence. But it was there. An easy silence of understanding.

"I like how you've aged."

Her comment had him laughing and then turning to look back out to sea.

"I'm serious," she said, lightly poking his side.

"Well, I'm glad." He grinned at her. "You've aged well too."

"Thanks." She pretended to fluff her hair and he snickered. "I will admit I've been staring at you quite a lot."

"Oh really?" he asked, his right brow hitching into his hairline.

"Not like that." She shoved his shoulder as he grinned.

"It's just... it's like I'm trying to see what's remained the same about you and what's different. I still see you as fifteen and it's been neat to see you now."

"I know what you mean."

"But I like you," she added, sizing him up with those devastatingly blue eyes that mirrored the ocean he loved so much. "I like the man you've become. At least, what I've seen so far. And I'm proud of you. Seeing you today on *The Voyager* was a treat. I got to see you as you are. Day in and day out, you're Captain Matt." She reached down towards the base of the bench and plucked a flower and began toying with it between her fingers.

"I felt that same way when I helped you at Bilbo and Mamie's moving stuff around. It was Olivia in action."

A cruiser sailed by and tourists waved to them, Matt and Olivia responding in kind. Olivia giggled.

"What's so funny?"

"People."

Furrowing his brow, he angled his body towards hers and rested his elbow on the back of the bench. "Care to elaborate?"

She pointed towards the passing boat. "There is absolutely no reason for them to wave at us. They can't see who we are from way out there, so they don't know us. It's just them saying, "Hi! Look at us! We're on a boat!" And then us waving and saying, "I know! That's awesome! Have fun!" Just humans being kind and friendly to one another."

"Hadn't thought about it like that, but you're right. A kind collaboration in their excitement. Boy, what would the world look like if we acted that way all the time?"

"Exactly my thought." Sighing, she stood, tossing the flower back into the grass. "I should head back to the store."

He glanced at his watch. "Yikes, and I need to head to the docks. I've got 45 minutes to get my act together before the next tour." He fell into step beside her as they made their way up the grassy incline and back towards the boardwalk. "You know, Liv, for what it's worth, I'm proud of you too."

Inclining her head towards him she smirked. "For what?"

"For turning out so great. With your parents' split and life taking you all over, you've seemed to find your place in life."

"Maybe. Though since being back here, I've begun to wonder if I have."

"You don't like living in Florida?"

"Yes and no. For the most part, it's great. However, I currently do not have a job there, remember? So my life will be a bit different when I head back. I've got to figure out my next move. And on top of that, I've realized just how much I've missed Friday Harbor. There's a piece of me here that I didn't know was missing. Like I left part of myself here and I've come to collect it." She shrugged her shoulders. "And perhaps I'll do just that, and when I leave this time, I won't be so heartbroken."

Not liking the turn in conversation, Matt pointed towards an alley way that allowed them a shortcut towards the back of Anchors Aweigh. He didn't want Olivia to already be thinking about life outside of Friday Harbor. He wanted her here. And while he had her, he was bound and determined to convince her to stay. There'd be no leaving a second time. He wasn't quite sure if his heart could handle her departure again. He did know, however, that he could not handle another fifteen-year separation. He didn't like the thoughts that idea conjured in his mind. He didn't like envisioning his life without her. And though he'd only had her back in his life a week, Matt was already feeling that connection they'd shared as kids. She belonged here. With him. And he only had a few short months to convince her of that fact.

« CHAPTER SEVEN »

Beth left the store after her expected customers came to pick up the chairs and table purchased earlier in the day. Promising a meal of shrimp, steaks, and tantalizing sides, she hurried out to make her way back to Lakedale, so as to have plenty of time to prepare for company. Olivia sat behind the register and keyed in receipts and balanced the till. Sales were up, as she hoped, and she now had to figure out a new window display. Thankful that she'd have a full day tomorrow to work on that project, she locked the money in the safe and headed towards the apartment to shower and ready herself for Matthew. Funny how just a few short days ago her life seemed completely off track. Since arriving in Friday Harbor, she hadn't focused on Orlando at all. In fact, she'd been so distracted by improving

Bilbo and Mamie's store, that she hadn't even checked her email for the last week. Not that there'd be anything important. She slid onto the edge of the bed and flipped her laptop open. A quick check to make sure all was fine with subleasing her apartment would be all she needed before jumping in the shower.

When she opened her email, her breath caught at the sight of her former boss' name.

Olivia,

I think decisions were made in haste. We'd like you to reconsider your departure. The position of regional visual coordinator is yours should you accept. Please contact me at your earliest convenience.

Stunned, she sat and read through the message several times before realizing that Cheyenne must have quit or been fired already and that was the only reason the job was extended her direction. That thought left a bitter taste in her mouth. Second choice was always hard to come to terms with when you had hopes of someone else. But she needed a job. She'd think on it. She wasn't sure if she wanted to go back to a company that did not see her worth or did not fulfill their promises. And right now, she had a great position at Anchors Aweigh. She had committed to helping Bilbo and Mamie until the end of August, and unlike her former company, she was determined to keep her word. She closed her laptop and stored it on her nightstand. Shuffling her way to the small and orderly bath, she took a full hour to prepare herself for an evening with the Summers family.

As she ran the brush through her hair one last time and touched up her lipstick, she heard the doorbell ring and knew Matt had arrived to pick her up. She closed the door to the apartment and headed towards the front of the store.

Matthew waved before sliding his hand back into his pocket as he waited for her to unlock the door. He wore jeans and a light blue t-shirt that matched perfectly with the white sundress with blue flowers she'd selected.

"Ready to go?"

She nodded as she turned to lock the door behind her and pocketed the key in her purse. He pointed up the boardwalk and towards a public parking lot. He clicked the button on his key fob and lights to a an open-topped Jeep flashed in welcome. "Hope you don't mind a little wind."

"Not at all." She snatched a hair tie from her wrist and drew back her hair. "I came prepared."

"Atta girl." He beamed as he opened the passenger door for her and hurried around to his own. The drive to his parents' house was too short in Olivia's book. The vast swath of spruce, hemlock, fir, and pine painted a forested stretch that opened up to a gorgeous two-story cabin overlooking Fish Hook

Lake. The Lakedale Resort could be seen further down the water's edge, but Matthew's parents had a beautiful spot to call their own. She could now see why his father worked closely with the resort. Matthew parked in a circle drive, gravel crunching under their feet as they headed towards the front door. The vast porch held comfortable furniture, robust plants and flower blossoms hanging from layered nets and climbing available trellises, and a vintage drink cart nestled to the side. Olivia noted the half empty rocks glass that looked to have held an adult beverage that someone had forgotten about. The condensation ring beneath it told her it hadn't sat unattended for long, no doubt Matt's father, awaiting their arrival, had left it behind when Beth rallied him to fire up the grill. The scent of which had Matt bypassing the front door and leading her around the side of the house to another sweeping porch, only this one attached itself to a beautiful deck overlooking the lake.

"Smells like they're upstairs." He nodded to a pinewood stairwell and traipsed up the stairs.

"There he is!" A deep voice greeted in welcome as Matthew reached the top. He stood to the side as Olivia finished the climb. "And there's Olivia." The man beamed as he shut the lid to his grill and walked towards them. He extended his hand. "Nice to see you again, Olivia. I know you probably don't remember me, but I'm Roy."

"Nice to see you as well." She shook his hand and watched as Matthew's dad gave him a fatherly pat on the shoulder. "Come on over. Beth ran inside to grab some drinks right quick and some appetizers. I just fired up the grill, so it will be a few minutes before we throw the meat on." He motioned towards the white wicker porch furniture with nautical themed cushions. "Have a seat."

Olivia accepted the cushion next to Matt as Beth emerged from behind them carrying a tray containing a fruity concoction she'd topped with slices of pineapple and cherry. She handed one to Matt and one to Olivia before helping herself. "I'm so glad we decided to do this," she said, as she smiled and reached over to squeeze Olivia's hand in welcome. "I was telling Roy about my day at the shop and how wonderful your displays look. Mamie will be thrilled when she gets back and sees what you've done with the place."

"That's my goal," Olivia added. "I've got a ways to go, but I have a plan. I'm hoping I can rope Matthew into helping me again. He makes a good worker."

Matt winked at her as he took a sip of his drink. "I was just a bystander keeping you company."

"Still a big help," Beth assured him. "Sometimes company makes the work go by faster."

"Exactly," Olivia agreed.

"Now, you're here until the end of August, right, Olivia?" Roy asked.

"That's the plan."

"Perfect time to be in Friday Harbor. Great fishing weather. Have you taken her out yet, Matt?"

"No sir. Haven't gotten that far."

"Sailing?" his dad asked.

"Not yet."

"Well, why not?" His dad looked utterly confused and Olivia bit back a grin as Matt just shook his head.

"She's only been here a week, Dad."

"Ah. Right. I see. Well, you have the whole summer to catch up then. That's nice." Roy toasted towards Olivia as he took a sip of one of Beth's drinks. He sputtered and choked on a cough. "My word, Beth, what'd you put in this thing? A whole bottle of vodka?"

"Is it too strong?" Beth's innocent expression had Matt and Olivia chuckling.

"I'd say so. It practically burned my insides. I think I'll stick to my scotch." He nodded towards a decanter sitting on top of a hand-hewn wet bar under the patio and Beth rose to fix him a drink to his liking.

"You two want something different?" Roy asked.

"They're fine, dear. They're young. They can handle a stiff drink." Beth winked as she walked her husband's glass over to him and then sat back in her chair.

The wind teased Olivia's hair and she realized she'd yet to remove the hair tie that housed her perky ponytail. She slipped her hand up and pulled it down, lightly brushing her fingers through her hair. Matt reached over and helped smooth flyaway strands and tucked them behind her ear. His parents watched closely.

"Now, you're in Florida these days, Olivia?"

"Yes sir." She smiled as she waited for Roy to continue.

"We went down to Florida, oh what was that, Beth? Three years ago?"

"Five, dear."

Roy shrugged as if the exact time frame didn't matter. "Destin area," he continued. "Pretty place. Pretty beaches. But boy, was it hot."

Olivia grinned. "It does get steamy down there. Humid and hot."

"And you like it?" he asked.

"Most days," she admitted.

Roy continued making conversation, asking about her parents and brother, about her latest design plans for the shop's interior, and about her tour with Matt earlier in the day. He carried the conversation while Beth and Matt exchanged small worried glances throughout the great inquisition. However, Olivia did not feel as if she were in the hot seat. She felt comfortable and at home. And relaxed. Though she credited some of that to Beth's liquid concoction. But the homey feeling she credited to Roy. He was kind, funny, and jolly, much like his son, and she realized Matt was a mirror image in temperament of his dad.

Beth stood to her feet. "Olivia, you mind helping me grab some snacks from the kitchen?"

"Not at all." Olivia set her drink on the glass-topped table and patted Matthew's knee in farewell as she rose and followed his mother into the house. She gasped when she walked through the French doors and into the open and airy kitchen.

Beth turned with a worried expression until she saw the awe on Olivia's face. "It's a dream kitchen, isn't it?"

"Very much so. It's beautiful." Olivia floated towards the quartz countertops and stared at the delicious spread Beth had prepared.

"I love it too. Roy outdid himself in here."

"He built this?"

"Oh no, dear." Beth laughed, holding a hand to her heart. "He designed it for me. See, Roy has an eye for design, much like you. He just seems to have a vision and can bring it to fruition. Poor Matthew inherited my genes. We have to see a finished product before we can fully understand the creative mind. But I told Roy I wanted a kitchen that allowed me to feel the outdoors, and he made it happen. The windows and doors leading out onto the patio allow me to see the lake and trees any time of day. It's quite refreshing."

"I bet." Olivia grasped the tray of cheeses Beth placed in her hands. "Puts my view in Florida to shame."

"Oh, do you have a beautiful view of the city?" Beth asked wistfully.

"Not quite," Olivia snickered. "A brick wall of the neighboring building. In fact, I rarely see the beauty of the city. I tend to work odd hours."

"That's a shame. I hope you take time to enjoy the view while you're here." She smiled softly as she picked up a plate of crackers.

"Oh, I plan to. In fact, Matthew took me to a spot today for lunch to do just that."

"Outlook Point?" Beth asked.

"Yes, how'd you know?" Olivia asked.

"He goes there quite a bit. Sits on that rickety old bench you two made that one summer. It's his thinking spot. And it has a wonderful view of the water."

"That it does. I can't believe that bench is still there after all these years."

"Well, it has to be there," Beth assured her. "It took you two an entire week to build it."

Olivia laughed. "The building didn't take that long. The smuggling supplies was the time commitment."

Beth grinned as she led the way back outside and paused. "Why, hi there, Jake." She set her tray of crackers on the table and gave Jake a hug, his eyes carrying over to Olivia as he sat in the spot Olivia had vacated. He waved. "We didn't know you were stopping by." Beth waved for him to sit back down and Olivia placed the tray of cheeses next to the crackers.

"Had to. I could smell the sweet scents of Roy's cooking and had to see what was happening." He chuckled as he reached for what had been Olivia's drink prior to his arrival. He helped himself, his brows rising at the stout flavor, but he leaned comfortably back against the couch cushion. Matt stood to offer his own seat to Olivia, but she waved him back down. She didn't really want to sit by Jake. Though he was friendly, she just didn't fully embrace his charming exterior. She eased onto a small stool near Roy's chair.

~

"Heard you two ladies talking about that old bench," Jake commented. "Man, remember our thievery, Matt? The things a young boy will do to impress a pretty girl... even rope his best friend into his crimes." He winked at Olivia. "Thought we almost got caught once, but Mr. Roy just waltzed on by."

Roy shook his head and eyed his son. "I knew what you two were up to. You wouldn't have gotten away with it if I had needed the supplies. But as luck would have it, it was just scrap materials. Though I can't say the same for the resort right now."

"What do you mean?" Matt asked.

"Oh, seems like there's been a few cases of things gone missing."

"First the houseboats, now the resort?" Beth shook her head in dismay.

"And Ramsey's," Matt added.

Concern had Olivia straightening. "What happened to Ramsey's?"

"Nothing too bad," Jake interrupted. "Just some of his fresh catches were stolen off the hooks behind the bar before he could get them processed and in the kitchen."

"Not too bad?" Matt asked. "It was a day's worth of fishing. And it wasn't just the bar's supply. It was Leeward's as well. Ramsey supplies them with salmon as well."

Jake shrugged. "Still, nothing drastic. Whoever is going around stealing is just being a nuisance. I don't think they mean to have a life of crime ahead of them. Bunch of teens would be my guess."

"Still, it *is* stealing," Olivia added. "And poor Ramsey. I feel bad for him."

"Soft spot for ol' Rams, Olivia?" Jake asked, his brow quirked and an amused smirk on his face.

"I like him," she admitted, and Matt smiled at her defensive tone towards Jake. A protective streak had her sitting ramrod straight, and Matt liked that she felt connected to Ramsey and viewed him as a friend.

"So, what plans do you have for tonight?" Olivia asked, turning towards Jake.

"Work, unfortunately. I'm the pizza man tonight. Fishing tomorrow. Can't take a day off like this guy can." He tossed a thumb towards Matt and Matt tried to keep a neutral expression, though annoyance clawed its way to the surface. Olivia's jaw tightened at his friend's response.

"He had four tours today," she reported. "That's a long day."

Jake held up his hands to ward off argument. "Whoa, I didn't mean anything by it. Just teasing him." He playfully punched Matt's shoulder. "Got you a defender, buddy."

Matt ignored Jake and met Olivia's cool gaze. Her patience was waning as well, and he removed the glass from Jake's hand and sat it on the table. "Best take it easy on that if you have to work tonight." His tone was light and friendly, and he hoped his friend would catch the signal that he was not invited to partake in their dinner plans. To his relief, Jake stood.

"You're right. I need to head towards the Harbor anyhow. Olivia, good to see you again. That dress is pretty." He winked at her as he shook Roy's hand and gave Beth a light hug. "I'll be seeing you guys around." He started towards the stairs and turned. "Oh, by the way... Olivia, if you're free on Tuesday evening, I'd like to take you over to Orcas Island. Thought we could hike up to Mount Constitution. Wasn't sure if you were able to do that fifteen years ago." He nodded his heads towards Matt, knowing full well that at fifteen, Matt would not have been allowed to sail himself to Orcas Island. Jake waited for Olivia to respond.

The silence stretched a moment and Olivia cleared her throat. "Oh, well... that sounds neat. I'll let you know."

Jake nodded in agreement. "See you then." He hopped down the stairs and once out of earshot, Olivia turned to Matt.

"What's Mount Constitution?"

"Neat place," his dad interjected. "A lookout that gives you great panoramic views of the islands and mountains."

"I see."

"Matt hikes up there every now and then." His mother nudged his hand to speak up.

"It's a beautiful spot. I'm afraid it makes Outlook Point look like child's play," he commented.

"Honey," His mother's voice carried to his father. "The grill."

His dad jumped to his feet. "Oh gee, I forgot. I got to visiting and forgot my purpose."

Olivia chuckled as he hurried over to man his position. Matt stood and disappeared into the kitchen, emerging with a platter of raw shrimp on kabobs and thick slabs of meat. He held it for his dad as his Roy's metal tongs gently laid them on the grill with a tantalizing sizzle.

"If we hurry and eat, we might could go for an evening sail," his mom suggested. "We have gorgeous sunsets here," she gushed.

"I bet." Olivia glanced out over the lake. "It's amazing up here."

She offered a warm smile towards Matt as he waited patiently for his dad to finish placing the meat. He couldn't wait to take Olivia out on a sailboat. Not only was he a way better sailor than he was at fifteen, he had a nicer boat. And he wanted her to see it. He wanted her to see him as she did back then when they sailed out on the water. She'd fully trusted him. Not just with her safety but her thoughts, her hopes, her dreams, and even her young heart. And whether it was wishful thinking or he was just plain acting ridiculous, he wanted her to do the same now.

He jerked to attention as Olivia stood and followed his mom towards the house. "Where are you two off to?"

"Fixing Olivia another drink. Jake downed the last one," his mom called over her shoulder as she opened the door to the kitchen, and they disappeared inside. He could still see them through the glass, and he watched as they laughed and chatted with one another in easy company.

"She's a lovely girl." His father's voice broke his stare and he cleared his throat.

"Yes, she is."

"Never thought she'd make it back here."

"Me either. Pretty crazy, huh?"

His father nodded as he raised the lid of the grill to check the status of their dinner and then closed it. "How's it been between the two of you? Seems like you've pretty much picked up where you left off all those years ago."

"Somewhat," Matt admitted. "I mean... Olivia is fantastic, and we still have fun together."

"And—" His dad prodded.

"And she's gorgeous," Matt added with a flush to his face.

His dad chuckled. "Fifteen years is a long time."

"That's the truth. I didn't realize how long until I saw her again. Time moves fast."

"You were pretty stuck on her back then, even after she left. Even as you've grown and matured."

"Dad—"

"Don't Dad me. I know what I see, and I know what I saw. You two were old souls back in the day. Connected, too. The oddest thing was seeing you two together all over the harbor. Bilbo and Mamie kept a watchful eye for us when we couldn't be there, but you and Olivia shared something rare. Not only friendship, but a deep connection that is hard to find. I sense it now too. It's still there, lingering under the surface."

"I'm not so sure about that," Matt confessed. "We've grown up, gone our separate ways, have careers. She has a life in Florida. Friends. Family."

"And?"

"I just don't see her giving that up."

"Do you want her to?"

Matt shrugged. "It's only been a week. A lot can happen in a few months. I'm not going to get my hopes up."

"But you want her to stay?" his dad challenged.

"I always wanted her to stay."

His dad patted his shoulder in understanding. "Then can I give you a piece of advice?"

"Sure."

"Don't let Jake take her up to Mount Constitution."

Laughing, Matt shook his head. "And why not?"

"One, Olivia doesn't want him to. Two, you don't want him to. And three, *you* should take her. She wants you to take her. I saw it on her face when she looked at you. And I saw the heat rise in yours when Jake asked her."

Matt rubbed the back of his neck and sighed. "We'll see. It's hard to navigate around Jake when he's set his mind on something."

"And if his mind is set on Olivia? *The Olivia*?"

"Why does everyone keep calling her that?" Matt wondered aloud.

"Oh son..." His dad laughed. "Because she was and always will be *your* Olivia. You staked your claim on that girl long ago. Even if she left and made a life in Florida, everyone would always know her as Bilbo and Mamie's granddaughter and *your* Olivia. Two peas in a pod you were. I'm just sad I didn't get to know her then. Would love to compare the young girl to the woman in there with your mom."

"They're pretty much the same, only now she seems... sweeter. Not that she wasn't sweet back then," he quickly amended. "She just seems... better than before?" He held up his hands and then ran them over his face, embarrassed at the turn in the current conversation and his lack of words.

His dad chuckled. "Nothing wrong with a wonderful girl growing up to be a wonderful lady."

Matt snapped his fingers. "There, let's go with that."

They both laughed as the women walked out carrying plates and utensils. "You better not overcook my steaks, Roy," his wife scolded.

"I haven't." His dad feigned a grimace as he opened the grill and quickly removed all the meat. "I hope you're hungry, Olivia," he called over his shoulder. "Beth's whipped up enough food to feed an army."

"I can't wait. It all looks and smells delicious." She looked to Matt and squinted. "You okay?"

"Of course." He stepped forward and took one of the two bowls in her hands and walked it over to the wooden picnic table his mother had dressed with napkins and place settings. She pointed to a spot and he set the decorative bowl where she ordered. Olivia walked up beside him and placed the dish she carried next to his. She linked her arm with his as they waited for his dad to bring the meat tray over. His mother bustled over with a fresh platter for him to place the meat, her hopes of having a delicious meal but pretty presentation as well. When she walked off, Olivia stood on her tiptoes and kissed Matt on the cheek.

Surprised, he glanced down at her smiling face. "What was that for?" he quietly asked.

"A thank you," she whispered. "For bringing me. I've enjoyed this."

"I'm glad." He rested his free hand over hers at the crook of his opposite elbow as they waited for his parents. "And tomorrow, if I can convince you not to work, we should hike to Mount Constitution."

Her brows rose.

"I kind of want to beat Jake to the punch."

She bit back a pleased smile as his mother walked up and motioned for them to sit. His dad joined them, and his mother held up her glass. "To old friends."

Matt felt Olivia squeeze his hand under the table as they clinked their glasses with his parents', and he brushed his thumb over her knuckles in response. It wasn't until his dad slapped a steak on her plate for her to cut into that she released her hold on his hand. Regrettably, he brought his hand up to the table to begin eating himself, but the warmth of her palm against his and the subtle way in which she acknowledged him during the toast, had his hopes slowly rising. Hopes he knew he shouldn't have, but that continued to taunt him.

« CHAPTER EIGHT »

Olivia slid her sandals off and walked them to the small armoire she used as her closet and made her way to the bath. It'd been a great evening with Matt and his parents. They'd eaten and chatted until the sun had disappeared over the horizon and the moon and stars took center stage in all their glory. She hadn't seen stars like that in a long time. She could still smell the night air coming off the lake, the lingering scent of steak and shrimp. She'd log it away as a special memory. No evening sailing, but the company and conversation was well worth skipping that activity. She hadn't felt that connected with a family in a long time. Sure, she had her own family, but she rarely saw her mom, and Henry had his own life happening in Portland. And her dad, well, he was in Louisiana. They all seemed to acknowledge they were family but didn't necessarily act like one. Unless a special occasion or a death happened, she thought. And how sad was that? Seeing Matthew interact with his parents warmed her heart. They respected each other and valued one another. And it was clear to see that Roy was Matt's best friend and vice versa. And that's what Olivia didn't have. Her mom was not her best friend. She didn't have one if she really thought about it. Not that she needed one. But once you become an adult aren't you supposed to have somewhat of a friendship with your parents instead of just a familial responsibility? She'd admit she wasn't the best about calling her mom. However, she did make time for calls to Mamie and Bilbo each week. She felt closer to them than anyone else in her family. Her relationship with her grandparents probably explained why the longer she stayed in Friday Harbor, the more she considered moving there.

Which was crazy. Wasn't it?

She still had the entire summer to think about it. Well, unless she replied to her former boss' email. Which she hadn't let herself worry about all evening and she wasn't about to start now. She wanted to bask in the joy of her night with the Summers family.

Olivia slipped into the steaming tub and sighed as she reached for the worn copy of *Moby Dick* she'd started reading again three days prior.

She blamed it on Ramsey's wood carving and Matthew's ability to recognize her quotes. Smiling, she thought of him. The quiet car ride back to the harbor. The fact neither of them spoke and yet the quiet of the night and the sound of his Jeep satisfied the lack of conversation. The wind in their hair. His eyes focused on the road while his hands rested lazily on the wheel as he drove. There was no rush back. There was just easy silence. And then, when he'd walked her to the shop's door, he'd insisted on walking her inside and towards the door to her small back apartment.

She thought he was going to kiss her. It was the perfect night to. But he didn't. He'd just flashed that Matthew smile, the one that even now had her insides dancing. He'd reached for her hand and kissed her knuckles.

Something had shifted between the two of them this evening. Was it old feelings peeking their way through? Was it new feelings rushing to the surface? Olivia closed her eyes and envisioned the evening in detail. Down to the shape of her glass, the feel of the silver utensils in her grasp, the first bite of shrimp that rested on her tongue. Every mental image had a taste and smell tacked to it. Even Matthew.

Olivia swished out of the bath and dried her damp skin before slipping into her most comfortable pajama pants and top, her book forgotten on the floor next to the tub. Yes, even

Matthew had a scent: salty seas and fresh air mixed with light traces of his musky soap.

She fluffed the pillow on her bed and crawled beneath the comfortable bedding, reaching over to tug the lamp string. The room went dark, except for the bright green numbers on the bedside alarm clock. It was almost two in the morning and she wasn't even tired yet. She didn't even bother setting the alarm. And, she realized, her cell phone was still in her purse on the other side of the room. Already cozy, she decided to leave the phone where it was and enjoy snuggling under her covers. Smiling in the dark, she rearranged her head on the pillows, gave them an extra fluff and beat with her hands so as to create a more comfortable position that might invoke sleep. But nothing worked. She was just too happy to go to sleep. Giddy, even. She'd curse Matthew tomorrow, but tonight she only thought of his best qualities and how lucky she was to cross paths with him again after so many years.

She closed her eyes and attempted counting sheep, but her mind was restless. Yawning, and praying that meant sleep was on its way, she nuzzled deeper into her covers, but bolted upright at the sound of glass breaking and clattering to the floor. She slammed her hand on the nightstand for her phone and realized it wasn't there. Muttering under her breath, she threw back the covers and tried to find her way towards her purse in the dark.

Scuffles could be heard through her door. She prayed the intruders did not test the lock on the apartment door as she silently fished her phone from her purse. She tapped the screen, but the lights did not flash on. Dead. Running a nervous hand through her hair, she contemplated sneaking out into the store to use the landline but knew there was no way she could make it there unseen, much less make a phone call. A crash pounded against her door as if a piece of furniture had slammed into it. She dropped her phone and hurried towards her bathroom. The small window above the bath was just wide enough for her to squeeze through. She unlocked the latch and shoved it upwards, climbing her way onto dirt and gravel that covered the alleyway. When she'd cleared the threshold, she sprinted towards the docks. Panicked, her feet pounded on the boardwalk as she neared the pier and the rows of boathouses. She tried to remember which one was Matt's and then spotted a small boat with various cables tied to poles and tin foil wrappings that seemed extraterrestrial. The neighbor in search of a stronger television signal, which meant the boat next to it was Matt's. She thudded onto his deck, slipping and banging her hip into a handrail. Hissing from the brief pain, she hurried to the small cabin door and pounded.

He didn't answer.

Pounding harder, Olivia began rethinking her decision of coming to the docks. The house boats were one of the locations the local thieves had been pilfering. They could be here now, or worse, had followed her. Her eyes darted to the silent boardwalk as she pounded her fist once more on Matt's door. It swung open to a bleary-eyed Matthew.

"Liv?" he asked, his voice groggy.

She shoved him inside and closed the door behind them, sliding the locks in place. More alert now, he eyed her with worry. "What's wrong?"

"Someone broke into the store," she whispered in a hushed tone, peeking through his blinds towards the boardwalk.

"You ran from the store?" His eyes widened as he gripped her shoulders and led her to a small chair crammed beside a cupboard. "Tell me what happened."

"I was getting into bed. Just laid down." She struggled to catch her breath as her heart continued to race. "I heard them break inside. My phone was dead. I snuck out."

He reached for his phone and immediately began dialing numbers. "Ramsey, it's Matt. Yeah, I know... sorry about the hour, but Anchors Aweigh was just hit. They might still be there." He hung up.

"Shouldn't we call the police?"

"We just did. Ramsey's brother is the sheriff."

"Then shouldn't we call him?"

"We did. He and Ramsey live together." He knelt in front of her and covered her hands in his. "Calm down, Liv. You're safe here. Ramsey will call when it's clear."

Her hands trembled in his. "What do they want with Bilbo and Mamie's place? Surely, they know there's nothing worth any real value there. It's just trinkets."

"It's a business. I imagine they were expecting to find money in the register."

"I locked it in the safe," she assured him and herself. Regret swamped her. "I'm going to have to call Bilbo and Mamie and somehow convince them not to cut their trip short."

"They'll understand. Bilbo was aware of the break-ins on the docks, so it may not come as too big a shock to him." Matthew eased onto the edge of his bed, the small cabin housing a bed, small table, and a shower off to her right. Tight quarters for a man as tall as Matthew. "You okay?" he asked, interrupting her perusal.

"I think so." She ran a hand through her hair, thankful it wasn't shaking anymore.

"You want some tea or coffee?"

"Sure." She watched as he walked towards the tiny half kitchen and set a kettle on the single burner.

His phone rang. "Ramsey," he greeted, his eyes turning towards Olivia. "She's fine... sure, we'll be over in a few minutes." He hung up and turned the kettle off. "Tea will have to wait. Ramsey and his brother are at the store and say it's clear. Ready?"

Olivia accepted the hand he offered, and he slipped into a pair of flip flops on their way out.

Walking up the boardwalk, the night was still quiet despite the small bustle of activity around Anchor's Away. When Ramsey spotted them, he headed their direction. He accepted Olivia's grateful hug as he motioned them towards the inside of the shop. "Reagan's inside. Doesn't seem like anything was taken, but you'd be the better judge of that." He nodded towards Olivia as she carefully stepped over the broken glass, her bare feet slightly chilled from the walk over. Once inside, her heart sank. Displays were tumbled over, a few items broken and scattered around the floor. Behind the desk, the register drawer was yanked free and the safe had several indentions from what looked like a crowbar or hammer. But the lock and door hadn't budged for the thieves.

"Must have given up." Matt said, his eyes taking in the mess.

A man as tall as the jolly green giant with a scraggly beard and a missing front tooth walked up. When he stood next to Ramsey, Olivia could immediately see the family resemblance. "Ms. Miles," he greeted.

"You must be Reagan, the sheriff." She shook his hand.

"Yes ma'am." He sent Matthew a clipped nod of welcome. "Sorry we meet under such circumstances. It doesn't appear they've taken anything. The door to your apartment wasn't tampered with, but they did give the store a thorough search. Once you've had time to really look around, let me know if anything was taken. Do you know if Bilbo and Mamie have security cameras? I didn't see any but wasn't sure if they would have them hidden somewhere."

"Not that I know of." Olivia nibbled her bottom lip as she wandered around the store, stepping over items and furniture pieces. Other than the damages to some of the inventory, she didn't notice anything missing.

"I've got a couple of deputies keeping an eye out for the rest of the night, but I doubt we'll see them. Did you hear anything other than the glass from the front door?"

Olivia shook her head. "Just sounds of them doing a bit of this." She waved her hand over the destruction. "And then I snuck out and ran."

"Smart girl." Reagan nodded his approval as he handed her a card. "If you need anything, let me know. We've got what we need, and I've got Handy bringing over a piece of plywood for the front door."

"Thanks, Reagan." Matt shook his friend's hand.

Ramsey gave a reassuring squeeze to Olivia's shoulder as he followed his brother out. When they were alone, Olivia looked to Matt in dismay, her eyes growing glassy. Matt stepped forward and enveloped her in his arms. "Don't worry, Liv. We'll get the place back in order. The good news is you are safe and nothing was stolen." She rested her head against his chest as he held her close. "Why don't you try and get some sleep? I'll wait for Handy."

Olivia swiped a hand over her cheek as she stepped out of his comforting embrace. "Not sure if I'll be able to sleep."

"I'm not going anywhere, so get some rest." He nudged her towards her apartment with a tired smile and Olivia felt the adrenaline of the night fade away as her body grew weary. When she spotted her bed, the sleep that so eluded her earlier came swiftly once her head hit the pillow.

~

Matt wiped his hand over his sweaty forehead before lifting the last of the trash bags into a wheelbarrow he'd borrowed from Ramsey. His dad slapped him on the back as he pushed it out the door, handing it off to Handy who'd take it to the dumpster. The door to the apartment opened and Olivia stepped out, her hair pulled back into a ponytail, her face clean of makeup and her hands tucked into her jean pockets. Her eyes widened at the sight of all the people in the store and the cleanliness of the previous disaster. His mother spotted her and rushed over, enveloping her in a big hug and giving a gentle rub between the shoulder blades meant to soothe. The touch only mothers seemed to master. Olivia's shoulders relaxed as his mom chatted with her, waving and pointing in different directions. Olivia's steady blue gaze found his and he smiled.

"You've been busy. Why didn't you wake me?"

"You needed rest," he said. "And all I did was call my parents. Everyone else just showed up to help when they heard about it this morning. Friday Harbor locals wake early, and when they found out what happened, they came in droves to help." He pointed to several helping hands Olivia vaguely recognized from the night they were at Ramsey's, and she knew her new friend had rallied his troops. Jake also stood amongst the crew and he offered a sympathetic wave as he went back to sweeping.

"I can't believe all the people that are here and the work you guys have gotten done. You should have woken me up."

"I figure you will have plenty to deal with today. At least this way, you're rested and have somewhat of a clean slate to work with. And you will have my mom, dad, and me to help with whatever you need us to do."

"First things first, I need to call Bilbo and Mamie." Olivia walked towards the landline and sat in Bilbo's chair behind the register. "Here goes nothing." She crossed her fingers and he gave an encouraging smile as he leaned his elbows on the counter to observe. "Bilbo?" Her face split into a smile at her grandfather's voice, but it quickly faded as her tone grew more serious. "I have some news."

Matt turned as his mother walked up and motioned for him to follow her. "Give her some space, honey," she whispered.

Matt flushed. "I just wasn't sure if Bilbo would want to talk to me or not."

"Why would he?"

"I don't know." Matt shrugged.

She smiled as she cupped his cheek. "You're a sweetheart, you know that?"

"Mom." He rolled his eyes as she grinned. "If Bilbo wishes to speak with you, she'll call for you, but until then, give her some time to chat with them and you can—"

"Matt?" Olivia's voice interrupted their conversation, and he gave his mom a smirk as she lightly swatted his arm. "Bilbo wants to talk with you." She handed him the phone.

"Hi Bilbo," he greeted.

"Hey there, Matt. Well, how bad is it?"

Sighing, Matt slipped into the chair Olivia vacated as she walked towards the back of the store to no doubt start pulling inventory to bring to the front. "It's not terrible. From what we can see, nothing was taken. They tried to break into the safe and when they couldn't, I guess they just gave up."

"Olivia told me what all happened. I hate that for her. Is she scared to stay at the store by herself?"

"Not that I can tell. Reagan has some extra patrols walking the boardwalk at night and has promised to keep those going with special stops near Anchors Aweigh. I don't think they'll be back now that there's been so much attention."

He heard Bilbo heave a heavy sigh. "Mamie is not going to like this."

"Bilbo, can I be straight with you a second?" Matt asked.

"Always, son. Always."

"The store lost some inventory, mainly due to breakage, but overall, I think it is fine. Olivia will be fine. She's brave. It shook her up, but she's already starting to order people around and get the shop organized and ready for business. She doesn't want you guys to cut your trip short. And neither do I, if I'm being honest. If you and Mamie come back, there is no reason for Olivia to be here. And to be honest, Bilbo, I'm not ready for her to leave."

He heard a soft familiar chuckle. "I wondered how you two were faring. I trust you, Matthew. If you think Olivia can handle the situation, then I will leave it in her hands. But, if at any point you feel she needs us, you will let me know."

"Of course. All my selfishness aside, if the store and Olivia need you here, I will definitely call you."

"Well, then it sounds like it is all in good hands. I hate that it happened, and that Reagan has no clue who's terrorizing the harbor. I'll email Olivia the insurance information just in case she needs it. But if it's just the front door needing repairs, I'd just as much prefer her just to replace it and not worry about insurance."

"I'll let her know."

"Thanks for being there for her, kiddo. We appreciate you."

"It's been one of my greatest pleasures, Bilbo. I should be thanking you for getting her back here."

"Take care and pray for me. For I've got to tell Mamie about all this."

Chuckling, Matt hung up.

"Well?" He jumped at the sound of Olivia's voice and turned. She stood with hands on hips as a pile of boxes stacked next to her feet.

"I've called off the hounds." He smiled. "They aren't coming back. They leave it in your capable hands. Bilbo said he's going to email you."

She heaved a relieved sigh. "Thank you."

"What are those?" He pointed at the boxes.

"Believe it or not these are orca figurines... but not the creepy clown ones."

"That's a relief. Did we somehow luck out and all the creepy clowns were smashed?"

"All but one." She giggled and then covered her mouth and grew serious. "I shouldn't be relieved about that, but I kind of am. I have no idea how I'm even going to sell the one."

"You will. Now, what do you want me to do?"

"I've got you an area set up over there." She pointed to a wall towards the rear of the store. "There's a few shirts that need to be folded and placed on the shelves. Just line them up under the correct display tee."

"Consider it done."

"And Matt?" He turned.

"Thank you, again."

"You're welcome." Pleased that she accepted the help of his family and himself, and pleased Bilbo trusted him with her care, Matt diligently worked to set the store to rights.

~

Jake, despite his annoying tendencies to hit on her every time she turned around, was kind. He'd helped most of the morning and disappeared close to lunch time only to reappear with pizzas for everyone to enjoy. She'd give him definite points for that act, but true to form, just a few short minutes later he was back hovering at her elbow to lay on his charms. It was rather exhausting really. Olivia hefted a glass sculpture onto a shelf. One of her favorite pieces in the entire store, a piece by the elusive artist known as F.W., Olivia made sure it was always a statement piece wherever she placed it. She'd already decided that if it had not sold by the time she headed back to Florida, she'd buy it for herself. Jake bumped her elbow, the sculpture wobbling on the edge of the shelf and in her hands. She reached up and righted the piece and gave a sigh of frustration. "Jake, could you just give me a minute, please?" Her clipped tone had his brows rising in surprise and his cheeks flushing as if he hadn't realized his attention was uncomfortable to her. Feeling remorseful for snipping at him, Olivia ran a hand over her face.

He held up his hands as he backed away, but his face split into a smile. "I'm crowding you and you need space to work."

"Sorry."

"No worries." He winked. "I've got to head to the restaurant here in a few any way."

"Thanks for your help," she called after him. He tossed a wave over his shoulder and she wasn't sure if she'd offended him or not. At the moment, she was only relieved he was finally out of her breathing space and even that thought made her feel bad.

"He'll get over it." Matt poked his head from around a clothing rack and his tilted smile had her relaxing. "He's just not used to a female not falling for his charisma."

Olivia groaned. "All morning he's been at it."

Laughing, Matt shook his head. "The store is looking great though, despite you being somewhat distracted."

"I didn't say I was distracted by it. Just annoyed," she pointed out. "But thanks. I may end up hiring your dad as well. Your mom said he had an eye for design, and he definitely does. He's pretty much taken over the entire back half of the store, and I am not disappointed."

"He'll be glad to hear it. So, at what point is the store actually done?"

"Never."

He chuckled. "That's what I was afraid of. Come on."

"What?"

He held out his hand and she eyed it warily. "Come with me."

"Why?"

He rolled his eyes on an exaggerated sigh. "Because I'm getting you out of here for a quick break. We'll come back and you can finish your little tweaks this evening. But right now, I'm kidnapping you and I'm going to take you sailing. We both need the break."

Suddenly aware that Matt had been up all night and all day helping her, his tiredness had her nodding. He needed the break, so she'd give him a break. He'd helped her more than anyone. "Alright, but your parents need to go and have dinner or something while we're gone. I don't want them to feel like they have to keep working while we're out enjoying ourselves."

"Mom! Dad!" he called, his voice causing both his parents' heads to pop up from behind shelving units like prairie dogs. Olivia grinned. "Break time. Go have some wine over at Leeward's for a bit. I'm taking Olivia sailing."

His mother stepped out, wiping her hands on her pant legs. "Now wine does sound lovely. Roy?"

Roy glanced at his work in progress and Olivia knew the struggle of leaving a project half finished.

"We'll get back at it later. I promise." She grinned as he winked at her in response and grabbed his wife's hand.

"Just holler at us when you're back. Take your time."

"Yes, enjoy the fresh air for a bit. You two look exhausted." Beth gave them each a hug as she and Roy walked out of the store hand in hand towards their favorite restaurant.

"See? Now everyone can take a breather." Matt beamed as he motioned for Olivia to walk out. She locked the door behind her and followed him up towards the docks.

"I will admit, being on the water for a bit sounds refreshing, but I know you have to be tired. Wouldn't you rather nap?"

Matthew pointed to a sailboat tied to the pier and Olivia gasped in pleasure. "Matt, it's beautiful!" She ran her hand over the bow as they began walking alongside it. "Far cry from what we used to sail in." She giggled as he extended his hand to help her climb aboard.

"I've had a few years to work on an upgrade." He grinned as she sat. "This Catboat was my first purchase about ten years ago. I have a Cutter as well, but since it's just the two of us, this one will be easier to handle."

Olivia shielded her eyes as she watched him prep by checking the lines and halyards. When he determined the wind direction, he raised the sails and attached them to the appropriate shackles on the boom. Olivia made a mental note to keep an eye on the boom. She vaguely remembered it swinging and popping her a few times when they, in their inexperience, had changed wind direction too quickly.

Before she knew it, they were starting their smooth departure out into the ocean. The wind caressed her face as she closed her eyes and let the sound of the water and the slap of wind against sail relax her. Matt was right, she needed this. She'd only sailed a few times in Florida over the years. It was her own fault too. She worked too much. She let work rule her life, displacing hobbies or outings on the water. The truth was, she didn't have anyone to sail with down in Florida. Her friends were her co-workers or former co-workers, and most had the same type of work schedule she did. Other than drinks during a happy hour now and then, that was the extent of her social life. But sitting now on Matthew Summers' sailboat, she realized that sailing was only fun when it was with him. As if he was the only person with whom it actually meant something. It was their thing. Wasn't it? After fifteen years apart, could she really claim that? He'd sailed over the years. So much so that he owned two sailboats. If not more. She watched as he finally sat and began to enjoy the ride. "I miss this."

He glanced her direction, his hazel eyes hidden behind his sunglasses. "Then perhaps you should get out more." He grinned.

"Right." She rolled her eyes. "I was just berating myself on that very thing."

"While you're in Friday Harbor, I will take you out anytime you want. All you have to do is ask."

"That's a generous offer. What if I said I wanted to sail every morning? Or every evening?"

"Then we'd go sailing."

"*Every* day?"

"If that's what you want."

She laughed in disbelief.

"One: I love being on the water, so you don't have to twist my arm on that. Two: I love being with you, so I doubt it would take much convincing to get me out here."

Silence hung between them and Olivia dipped her hand to the side of the boat to feel the splash of waves against her palm. Did he really mean what he said? It seemed he did. Matt was never one to tiptoe around his feelings. In fact, long ago he was the first to confess his heart. Olivia was too baffled and in disbelief to think a good-looking guy like Matthew had liked her. But he had. And according to him, he'd loved her. Even though they were young, innocent, and completely unaware of life's twists and turns, he'd loved her. And that feeling of pure acceptance was something she'd never felt since. And she wondered what it would be like to have that kind of love now, especially from a man like Matthew.

"I'm going to take us up towards Orcas Island. We won't dock or anything, but it's a pretty area."

"Sounds good to me." Olivia watched as a handful of porpoises passed by and eagerly accepted the waves the boat created. She pointed and Matt flashed a smile. "It's your buddies, Captain Matt."

He laughed. "I can't go anywhere."

Grinning, Olivia watched as the friendly creatures dove deep within the water and back to the surface again. She was almost close enough to touch them. The thought thrilled her. Perhaps, if she and Matt did start sailing every day, she might just get the opportunity.

« CHAPTER NINE »

Time had a funny way of sneaking up on him when he least paid attention to it. And before Matt could blink, a month and a half of having Olivia Miles back in Friday Harbor had passed. Anchors Aweigh had bounced back after the break-in. And Bilbo, in reviewing the sales from Olivia's previous weeks, gave Olivia free rein to restock the store with inventory of her choosing. She hadn't strayed too far from Bilbo and Mamie's style, but the small store had blossomed. Olivia had bowed her head and worked tirelessly to redesign the store layout and achieve impressive sales numbers. She'd succeeded at both, and in the process had been somewhat elusive outside of working in the shop. Sure, Matt stopped by with lunch periodically, but it wasn't the same as stealing her away for a few hours to accompany him on a tour or to go sailing. Her date with Jake never happened due to her all-consuming task of resetting the store. And Mount Constitution taunted Matt each day he passed by Orcas Island, because she had yet to even accompany him to the impressive lookout. When he woke up that morning, spotting her through the glass as he walked towards the docks, he was determined to change that. Now that his tours were done for the day, he was going to sweep her away. The bell above the door, new and somewhat less annoying than the old one, rang as he entered the shop. Olivia glanced up with a welcoming smile.

"Hey there. What brings you by this time of day?" She glanced at her watch and her face blanched. "Wow. I didn't realize it was already quittin' time." She grinned and pointed to the sign on the door and he flipped it for her.

"Is that Matt?" His mother's voice drifted from the back as she walked into the room carrying a fresh stack of reusable totes. "Hi, sweetie." She kissed his cheek as she walked towards a hanging rack next to the register. "Need a tote?" she asked. "We can't seem to keep them on the hanger, they sell so fast."

"I'm good, Mom. Thanks." He heard Olivia giggle as Beth just shrugged and set about arranging the totes. "I actually came to see if Olivia was up for dinner."

Her brows rose. She glanced at her watch again. "Leeward's will be packed, and it's probably too late to grab a table. Maybe Ramsey's?"

He shook his head. "I've something else in mind."

"Oh?" Olivia and his mother asked at the same time. He flashed a semi annoyed glance at his mom before looking to Olivia. "Pick you up in an hour?"

He watched her fumble for words. "Well— I was going t— an hour is fine," she finished.

"You sure?" he asked.

"Yes. I can be ready. Should I dress up or anything?"

"No. What you're wearing is fine."

"Oh. Okay." He thought he heard disappointment in her tone but realized he would be doing her a favor by telling her the date was casual. He knew she probably wouldn't want to hike in heels. "Where are we going?"

"It's a surprise."

She placed her hands on her hips. "You know I don't like surprises."

"Do I know that?" He held a finger to his chin in thought. "Maybe I forgot."

"Matthew Summers." She started walking towards him and he hurried out of the store with a quick grin of satisfaction as he watched her give up her chase. Now, he needed to organize his boat.

He was punctual. Always had been. So when he knocked on the glass of the storefront, his mother answered. "You're still here?" he asked.

"Yes. I'm working. Olivia wanted to make sure we restocked all the impulse items up near the register before we called it a day. You'd be surprised how many kids come by to check out the trinkets in the morning. It also keeps them occupied while their mothers shop."

"I see. Good to know. Liv ready?"

His mother shrugged. "I haven't seen her. She's pretty worn out, sweetie. I hope you don't have a big evening planned."

His excitement waned a touch, but he just shook his head. "Just dinner."

"Good. She's been working so hard lately."

"I've noticed."

His tone had his mom surveying him. "Are you upset with her?"

"No."

"You sound like you are," she pointed out.

"I'm not." He tucked his hands in his pockets.

"Don't lie to me, Matthew. I am your mother."

He smirked at that and she crossed her arms waiting for the truth.

"I just realized today how quickly time goes by... her time here in Friday Harbor. I haven't spent much time with her the last few weeks and I want to make sure I spend as much as I can with her while she's here."

"I see." His mom's tone still held a touch of disbelief.

Saved by Olivia, Matt watched as she emerged from the apartment. "Beth, you're still here? Go home." She gave his mom a hug before turning to him. She wore a light sweater the same color as her eyes and he felt his heart drop to his knees. "You look beautiful."

"I'm just in a sweater and jeans." She chuckled nervously as Beth shooed them towards the door.

"I'll lock up," his mother announced as she all but shoved them outside. Olivia turned to share one last thought, but his mother had already closed the door, offering an overly enthusiastic wave.

"What's she up to?" Olivia asked.

"I think she's just excited to see you taking a break."

"Hey now." Olivia squinted up at him. "Is that the pot calling the kettle black?"

"I'm done with work the same time every day."

"I have had a bit of tunnel-vision lately. It's just, with Bilbo and Mamie coming back next week, I want to make sure the store looks perfect."

He stopped in his tracks. "Next week?"

"I didn't tell you?" She held a hand to her forehead. "Sorry, I thought I had. Yes, they are headed back. They've made their rounds and Bilbo said Mamie was getting a bit road weary. They'll be here on the Sunday evening ferry."

"Wow. So, what does that mean for you?"

"Not sure yet. I'll probably stick around a couple of days to explain some of the changes I've made. After that, I'm not sure. My old boss emailed me a few weeks ago that the position I was promised could be mine if I came back. He's emailed twice since, which makes me think he is quite desperate. So, I may have that when I go back."

"I see. Well, it's a good thing I stole you away this evening."

"Why's that?"

He motioned to his sailboat. "Because we're going to Mount Constitution."

"I thought you said we were going to dinner?"

"We are. Up at the mount. Come on. Hop on." He was already tugging the lines when she climbed aboard. "For a woman who wanted to sail every day, you've been supremely slacking."

She laughed. "I've been busy, Summers. Cut a girl some slack."

"No way." He laughed as she dipped her hand in the water and tried to splash him. "I've got you for four more days, Olivia Miles. We are going to sail every single day you're here. Count on it."

His words sobered her expression as they drifted away from the dock, and she remained quiet for most of the ride towards Orcas Island. When he'd tied off the boat, he motioned towards her to follow him. They walked through the Moran State Park arch and wound their way through a series of trails. "We have a way to go, but I promise you it's worth it."

"I'll trust you." She was a smart hiker, placing her feet where he'd previously stepped. She didn't complain, and he barely heard her breathing. Earlier in the day, he'd been in such a rush hiking up to the mount, he panted his way up and down the trail. When they reached the top, he was pleased to see that his efforts were not wasted. Not a tourist in sight, just as Reagan had promised. Yes, he'd called in a few favors to make sure the lookout would be free from interruption. He'd wanted a peaceful, memorable experience for Olivia. And himself, if he were being honest.

"Wow. Are we the only ones here?" She looked around and spotted a small table with two chairs. The table was formally dressed. "Matt?" She looked to him and he grinned.

"I told you I was taking you to dinner."

"But up here? Is this… legal?"

He laughed. "It is for tonight."

Her mouth agape, she walked closer to the table and then looked up and out. She gasped, her hands covering her mouth as the gorgeous views swept her away from dinner and towards the ledge. "This is incredible."

"Thought you might like it."

"I love it. Wow, look at that." She pointed to the sea spray from what could only be orcas as the pod swam about.

"Here, come sit down." He pulled out a chair and she sat, still staring out over the horizon.

He lit an oil lamp on the table and then walked over to a small cart. Opening the lid, he retrieved two covered dishes and brought them to the table. He placed one in front of Olivia and the other at his place setting. He retrieved more dishes and placed them as well. He reached into the ice bucket and pulled out the bottle of wine that he was happy to see had chilled perfectly despite sitting in the sun for a couple of hours, thanks to his mother's trick of rock salt mixed with the ice.

Olivia watched him in stunned silence as he poured her a glass of white wine. When he handed it to her, she captured his fingers longer than necessary. "Matthew..."

He slipped his hand away, poured his own glass, and set the bottle back into the bucket. He toasted towards her. "To old and lasting friendships." Their glasses clinked and Olivia eyed him over the top of her glass as she sipped. He clapped his hands and rubbed them together. "Now, we feast."

Laughing, she lifted the lid to her dish and leaned back in her chair. "You've got to be kidding me!"

"It's just one of many appetizers."

"They're perfect." She plucked the first cheese stick off her plate and dipped it in sauce before popping it into her mouth.

"You happy, Liv?" Matt asked, hoping he'd given her a lasting memory of their time together.

"Very much so." She reached across the table and squeezed his hand, her eyes watering as she leaned over and kissed his cheek. "Thank you."

~

He'd planned a complete feast and she'd never felt so full in her entire life. Wine. Cheese sticks. Oysters. Shrimp. Lobster. Chowder. Fresh bread. Everything she loved from Ramsey's and Leeward's prepared in perfect portions for the two of them. She recognized the china dishes from one of Beth's kitchen cabinets and made a mental note to thank his mom for her contribution.

"When did you start working on this?"

"Earlier today. I wrapped up early and thought it was a great day for it. Beautiful weather. Beautiful views. And I missed you."

"You saw me yesterday," she pointed out, feeling a satisfied flutter in her stomach when he shrugged.

"I didn't know you were about to leave, but I'm glad I decided to do this now. Hopefully, it will give you fond memories of Friday Harbor when you think about us."

Her smile fell at the thought of leaving and her heart betrayed her again with thoughts of staying. Did Matt want her to stay? And why was that the only thing holding her back? She loved Friday Harbor, with or without Matt. She mentally scoffed at her thought and knew that one of the only reasons she loved the place was *because* of Matt. And if she decided to stay, he would be one of the reasons why. Yes, Bilbo and Mamie and the store ranked up there too, but her heart was tied to Matt. *Always had been*, she realized. And leaving him again would be hard. However, her life was now in Florida. And the job offer was still there. A job she'd worked years to achieve. She would be a fool to pass that up.

Matt reached for her hand and led her to a blanket and sat. Together they looked out over the sea. "Best view of the sunset that I could think of."

"I'd say you chose well." Sighing, she leaned back on her hands and stared up at the evening sky. "It's going to be hard leaving this place." She heard Matt's disapproving growl. "You know I have to, right?"

"No, I don't."

Surprised, she looked at him, his hazel eyes full of disappointment.

"My life is in Florida."

"And?"

She shook her head, bewildered that he did not see her viewpoint. "Well, I have an apartment there. I potentially have the job I've always wanted."

"And will both of those things make you happy?"

His question stung but she nodded. "I've worked hard for that position."

"I'm sure you have, Liv. But at the end of the day, are you happy?"

"How am I to know if I haven't taken the position yet? I think I need to at least give it a shot." Feeling defensive, she took a sip of her wine.

"I'm not trying to upset you. Trust me, that's the last thing I want to do."

"I know you're not," she whispered. "And it's a valid question. One I've been asking myself since I've been in Friday Harbor." She felt his fingers brush her cheek as he tucked her hair behind her ear to see her face better.

"I know Bilbo and Mamie will be sad to see you leave. As will my parents. Ramsey. Jake."

"And you?" she asked, turning to find him closer to her than she realized. His hand gently cupped her cheek as he tilted her face up to his.

"I'm surprised you even have to ask." He lightly brushed his lips over hers, testing the waters. Olivia's heart leapt and began to race as his lips lightly grazed hers again in question. She'd wanted this to happen since she first saw him again. This moment. This perfect opportunity to explore their friendship's boundaries. She answered his kiss and he tenderly held her face in his strong hands. Achingly sweet, Olivia felt the years fall into place. Their first sloppy kiss on the back of a beat-up sailboat had set their hearts in motion to this very moment. Matt had held her heart since she was thirteen years old and slowly, she felt her heart breaking much like it did back then. She'd have to leave him. And she knew she would. She had to give herself a shot at the dream job she'd worked hard to achieve. He'd understand. Sure, they'd both be sad to see the other leave, but they'd go about their own separate ways again and eventually they'd be fine. She pulled away from Matthew and placed her hand over his racing heart. "We should go now."

The mount was quiet. The entire island was quiet. And silence hung between them.

"Liv—" he began.

"Don't." She held her fingers over his lips. "Let's end the evening on a good note."

He pulled back as if she'd slapped him. Confusion marred his forehead before he stood and began storing the remnants of their dinner into the large cart to the side. She began carrying dishes over and he waved away her help. She'd hurt his feelings. She hadn't intended to, but one of them had to be realistic. "You can grab the blanket and tuck it in here as well. I plan on coming up in the morning to gather everything up."

"I can help you carry it down now," she offered.

"No. It's fine. We should go." He walked over and grabbed the blanket off the ground on his own, quickly folded it and stuffed it into the cart.

The trek down was always faster than the climb up, and Olivia was rather grateful for that since Matt had given her the cold shoulder. She didn't blame him. She was sad too. But the facts were the same. Her life was in Florida. Not in Friday Harbor.

The night sky above the quiet ocean was beautiful. She watched as Matt expertly guided them back towards the docks, his face devoid of any emotion. She'd think him perfectly fine were it not for his eyes. They were as stormy as the very sea they sailed when it had a mind to brew. His shoulders had yet to relax and his movements were stiff as if he were holding back his anger. She didn't want him to hold back. She didn't want either of them to have any unsaid words or regrets once she was gone. When they docked, she hopped onto the pier and waited for him, knowing full well that, though he was mad at her, he was still a gentleman and would walk her home.

True to form, he began leading her up the boardwalk. The streets were still buzzing with tourists enjoying the clear night and the view the boardwalk offered of the water and stars. Laughter and chatter could be heard from Leeward's deck tables and a hint of rowdy music drifted down the alleyway from Ramsey's.

"Are you not going to talk to me?" she asked.

Matt stopped and turned to her. "What is there to say? I want you to stay. You know that. You've decided to leave. What else is there to talk about?" He turned to head back towards Anchors Aweigh.

"Matt." She sighed, running a hand through her hair. "Come on. Don't be like this."

"Like what? Disappointed? Sorry, I am."

"That's not what I meant." Olivia reached for his arm and he took a step back to avoid her touch. Impatience had her resting her hands on her hips. "This is ridiculous. We are adults now. I'm sorry I can't stay in Friday Harbor. My life and my work are in Florida." Her voice began to rise, and several faces turned their way.

"It doesn't have to be, does it?" he asked, countering with an annoyed tone to match.

"I've worked years for this position." She held her hands out to her sides in exasperation.

"Then I'll move to Florida. If that's what it takes."

"I could never ask that of you. Your life is here. That'd be even crazier."

"No, Olivia, what's crazy is that fifteen years ago I fell in love with a bright-eyed girl who loved the sea. She loved adventure. She loved her family. And she loved me. What's *crazy* is that fifteen years later I find, in a surprising turn of events, that I am *still* in love with the bright-eyed girl who loves the sea, adventure, and family. The only depressing thought is that she obviously doesn't love me in return." He began walking towards the shop, several bystanders standing completely still to see what unfolded. Customers on Leeward's deck watched in stunned silence, Beth and Roy amongst them.

"You can't just walk away, Matthew," Olivia called after him.

She saw him take a deep breath as he turned. "I love you, Olivia. Always have and I always will. There's nothing more to say." And with that, she watched him continue past the shop and turn out of sight.

« CHAPTER TEN »

Matt went back to his schedule of mornings spent fishing for Handy and orca tours during the day. He ate lunch on his houseboat or over at his parents' house, neither of whom had brought up their presence at his recent love confession on the boardwalk. For that, he was grateful. He knew it was only a matter of time before his dad confronted him about it, but in the meantime, Matt enjoyed his solitude. He needed to come to terms with Olivia's departure, though it wouldn't be for another couple of days. Bilbo and Mamie were expected to arrive on the evening ferry, and he'd greet them with open arms and a cheerful smile. It wasn't their fault their granddaughter had broken his heart. Again. And this time, he would nurse it better than his fifteen-year-old self had done. He'd man up and face it head on. She was leaving. She didn't want him following her. Done. If that didn't give a man closure, then what would?

"I thought I might find you here." His mother's voice carried towards him as she and his dad worked their way up the dock. He rested his hands on the top of his mop handle. The half-finished deck on his boathouse would have to wait. The dreaded conversation he expected with his dad had arrived, and with it, his mother.

"Looks good, son." Roy stepped onto the boat first and then held a hand to his mother. They made their way to the deck chairs and sat, his mother crossing her ankles and leaning into his dad's side. Their affection for one another always touched him, and he was thankful he came from a loving home.

"What brings you two out here?"

"Oh, it's a lovely day. We also wanted to greet Bilbo and Mamie when they arrive." His mom checked her watch. "We still have a couple of hours, but we just didn't want to be cooped up at the house. We popped in on Olivia." His mother's leading tone had him quickly dipping his mop into the bucket and continuing his work. "Thought she might need some help, but she's decorated the store so lovely and then added some 'Welcome Home' decorations for the two of them. She must have been in her apartment because the door was locked, and I didn't see her through the window."

"That's nice."

"Oh, come on now, Matthew," his mom scolded. "Don't make me try so hard."

He heard his dad bite back a laugh as Matthew looked to his mother. "What is it, Mom?"

"The poor girl is miserable," Beth reported. "And I know you are too. Why are you avoiding one another?"

"I'm pretty sure you were there and should know."

"But why have you given up?" his dad asked. "You love the girl."

"It doesn't matter, Dad. She doesn't love me."

"That's ridiculous." His dad and mom shook their heads in dismay.

"Well, she didn't exactly confess her love to me the other night after I laid my heart at her feet. I don't think I need a clearer answer than that."

"She didn't mean it," Beth insisted. "She's just trying to be logical."

"Yeah, well, that's the problem."

"Of course it is," she agreed. "You have to convince her to stay. To see reason."

"She won't see reason, Mom. She thinks I'm the one being unreasonable. Actually, I believe 'crazy' was the word she used at the time." He pushed the mop over the planks and then tossed the dirty water over the side of the boat. "Listen, I appreciate the two of you worrying about me. But I will be fine. I'm already fine. I'm dealing with it."

"I don't know what in the world has happened, Beth, but our son has just completely lost his mind." Roy looked to his wife with concern. "Matthew, you listen to me. When Olivia left all those years ago, you were devastated. Completely heartbroken. And your mom and I always wondered why you hadn't settled down yet. But when you brought Olivia over to the house that night, we knew why. That girl has held your heart since you were kids. And she holds it now. But don't think you're powerless in this scenario. You hold hers as well. And if both of you bury your heads in the sand and let this chance pass you by, you're both going to wind up miserable." He patted his thigh like a judge banging a gavel. "Come, Beth, let's leave him to stew about this some more."

He heard his dad murmur something about "dumb kids" and "wasting their lives away" on his way off the boat, but nothing they could say would change his mind. Olivia had made her decision and it wasn't him. And this time, she actually could make the decision to stay on her own. The decision was in *her* hands, but she still did not choose him. That was answer enough.

He glanced around his boat and realized he'd scrubbed it from top to bottom and needed to move onto another task to keep himself busy. He thought about settling in at Ramsey's for an hour or so until Bilbo and Mamie arrived, but he wasn't in the mood for Ramsey's babble either. By now, the entire harbor knew of Matthew's rejection and he just wasn't in the mood for sympathetic looks or conversations about his heart. People needed to just leave it alone. He grabbed a cap and flopped it on his head. He'd go over to Lookout Point and sit for a bit. If he was going to "stew", as his dad put it, then he wanted to be in his favorite spot.

He waved as he passed by Ramsey's and felt a rush of relief that the bench was empty when he arrived. He'd had a brief sinking feeling that Olivia would be sitting there. But she wasn't. Instead, there was a white envelope with a rock on top of it. His name was scrolled across the front and he picked it up to sit. Unfolding the paper inside, he read:

Matthew,

Or Matt, I should say...

I'm sorry we had such a falling out the other day. I've missed you the last couple of days. Our friendship. It's odd, writing this short letter when I feel I have so much more to say, but this will have to suffice. I've already left, and therefore, these are the only words I will have to share with you.

I decided to leave on the noon ferry and meet Bilbo and Mamie at the ferry terminal instead of here in Friday Harbor. I figured it was best not to drag out the farewells or silences any longer.

Believe it or not, I am going to miss you. I've loved spending time with you and seeing the man you've turned out to be. You're everything I'd hoped you'd be and more.

Please, tell your parents goodbye for me. I've loved having your mom as my co-worker and friend. And your dad is a wonderful man. I've enjoyed getting to know them.

I'm sad to leave the harbor. I think back to that summer and the final farewell we shared on the pier. You were my best friend. My confidante. And I loved you. Seeing you again after all these years was like seeing a part of myself I'd lost long ago. A piece of my heart had been missing, and I hadn't realized it was here in Friday Harbor. I'm leaving it again now.

I hope you will remember me fondly. And that, should I make my way to Friday Harbor to visit, we will share each other's company with kindness and warm thoughts. Until then...

Olivia

Matt wadded up the letter and tossed it onto the ground. It sat a moment and he reached for it, undoing his damage, and read it again. She'd already left. No goodbye. No last hug or word. She just left.

He inhaled a shaky breath and covered his mouth with his hand at the sheer pain that sliced through him. He cleared his throat and bit back his emotions. There was nothing he could do now. Olivia Miles, *The Olivia*, was gone. Again. And this time, he wasn't sure if his heart would ever mend.

~

"Well, isn't this a nice surprise." Mamie, arms outstretched pulled Olivia into a tight hug, swaying back and forth before releasing her into Bilbo's arms.

"What are you doing here, Peach? Thought you were going to meet us on the boardwalk?" His eyes flashed to her suitcases and his face fell. "Oh no. Already?"

"I'm afraid so. That promotion opened up after all, so I'm headed back to Florida."

"Oh, I hate that." Mamie held a hand to her heart. "I was hoping we could hear all about your summer."

"I know. I'm sorry." Olivia grimaced. "It was time though."

Bilbo crossed his arms. "This wouldn't have anything to do with Matt would it?"

Shock registered over Olivia's face as she blushed from tip to toe. "Bilbo, no. Why would you even think that?"

"Beth and Roy called us."

Olivia's mouth dropped.

Bilbo chuckled as he tapped her chin. "Don't be so surprised. We've been chatting with them weekly since we left. They're our best friends."

"I guess I didn't realize—"

"That we had spies?" Mamie winked as she nudged Olivia to a small bench as they awaited their turn to board the ferry. "From what Beth has told me, you and Matt had pretty much picked up where you guys left off."

"Kind of," Olivia admitted, feeling oddly unsettled that Bilbo and Mamie possibly knew of her and Matt's last farewell.

"Well, I hate to see you jetting off so quickly." Mamie continued. "Thought we'd get you to ourselves a couple of days."

"I'm sorry," Olivia repeated. "It's just this job is what I've been working so hard for. Now that I actually have it, I don't want to miss the opportunity."

"Work isn't everything, Peach," Bilbo cut in.

"Bilbo—" Mamie warned. "We said we weren't going to get involved."

"And I'm not," Bilbo assured her. "Just know that should you decide to stay in Friday Harbor, the shop is yours."

"Wait, what?" Olivia's eyes felt as if they were going to burst from her head. "What do you mean mine?"

"Your Mamie and I discussed it long and hard over the last month and we plan to retire. We thought, if you liked it in Friday Harbor enough, you might like to take over the store. If not, then we'll just sell it. Might take some time to find the right buyer, but I think with the improved sales numbers and inventory you've brought us, it might set us up as a good buy."

"Bilbo, you can't sell." Olivia held her hand to her heart as she felt a wave of panic hit her chest.

"Why not? We've worked that store for forty years. Sometimes chapters close and it's on to something new." He squeezed Mamie's hand.

"But where will you live?"

"Oh, now that's the beauty of it. Your Mamie and I have a small cabin near Fish Hook Lake. We've talked for years about moving there full-time, but we worked at the store and it just made sense to stay in the apartment."

"I can't believe this." Olivia took four deep breaths, counting between each one to calm herself. If Bilbo and Mamie sold Anchors Aweigh, then the Friday Harbor Olivia knew and loved would disappear. First Matt. Then the store. She didn't think she could handle another loss.

"Honey?" Mamie asked. "You alright?"

"I can't do this." Olivia slouched against the back of the bench, Bilbo flanking one side of her while Mamie sat on the other.

"Can't do what, honey?" Mamie prodded.

"I can't leave Friday Harbor."

"Oh, now don't let us ruin your big plans and promotion." Bilbo squeezed her hand, though his eyes, with a gleam, flashed towards Mamie. "We aren't guilting you into anything, are we? Because honestly, we've thought about selling the store for years. It just hit us this trip that maybe we should offer it to you since you've handled it so well and seemed happy at the harbor."

"It's not just the store, Bilbo."

"Oh?" His brows rose.

She covered her face with her hands and her shoulders began to shake. A quiet sob broke through and Mamie pulled her into a hug. "Oh now, sweetie, it's okay."

"No, it's not." Her words were muffled against Mamie's shoulder. "I love him."

Chuckling, Mamie stroked her back. "And that's a bad thing?"

"No." Another sob and Mamie winked at Bilbo over Olivia's shoulder. "I was so cruel to him." Olivia pulled back wiping her eyes. Bilbo handed her a tissue that looked to have already been used, but she didn't complain. Dabbing beneath her eyes she began telling them of the night at Mount Constitution and Matt sharing his feelings for her on the boardwalk and how she shut him down. "I was so stubborn and stupid. I saw that my words hurt him, and I still denied my feelings and didn't tell him how I felt."

"It's never too late, Peach." Bilbo patted her knee. "Come back with us. I guarantee he'll be waiting for us at the dock."

"Oh, I couldn't possibly face him now." Olivia sniffled and Bilbo laughed. Mamie shushed him, but he continued to chuckle. "Don't be silly, Olivia. He loves you. All he wants is for you to come back. I'd bet a million dollars on that."

Olivia looked to Mamie and her grandmother tenderly straightened her hair and cupped her face. "Do you truly love him?"

Olivia nodded and a watery smile settled on her face. "Then a job should not stand in the way of you being with the person you love, Sweetie. Now, come on. Let's buy you a ticket for the ferry." Mamie grabbed her hand and began leading her to the ticket counter as Bilbo began shuffling their bags onto a cart.

Olivia looked at the ferry boat and prayed that this trip to Friday Harbor would be the last.

~

"There's Bilbo," Beth called, holding up a hand to wave. She saw Mamie step out behind him and then her heart soared at the sight of Olivia. Matt had yet to arrive but had said he was on his way last she spoke with him.

"Is that—"

"It sure is." Beth gripped her husband's arm and grinned. "She's come back, Roy. She's come back." She squealed and he held up his hand to calm her. "Easy Beth, we don't know why she's come back yet. It may have been her intention to travel with them in the first place."

"Not according to the letter Matt found. She'd said goodbye." She all but danced beside him as Mamie walked forward and gave her a hug. "I see you brought a stowaway," Beth whispered.

Mamie patted her back. "It would seem we have a new resident of Friday Harbor." The women pulled back to arm's length and grinned.

Beth pulled Olivia into a tight hug. "It's so good to see you. I already missed you."

Olivia chuckled as she struggled with her emotions. Her eyes searched the boardwalk for Matt, but he wasn't there. Emotions swam to the surface. Beth stepped back and quickly helped Olivia swipe the tears from her cheeks. "Not yet, honey. He's on his way. I promise you." She kissed Olivia's cheek, and when she stepped back Olivia froze.

Matt's joyful smile of welcome to Bilbo slowly faded as he spotted her. The older man's outstretched hand was forgotten as Matt walked towards her. Conversation died and everyone held their breaths as they waited to see what unfolded.

"I love you," Olivia blurted out and then nervously covered her mouth as she began to cry again. "And... I'm so... sorry for even think-thinking I could leave you."

Matt stepped forward and removed her hand from her lips and held it in his own. He lifted Olivia's chin to look into the eyes that had haunted his dreams for fifteen years. Eyes he'd grown to love even more now that they were focused on him.

"I love you," she whispered again with more conviction. "I always have. And I always will."

He pressed his lips to hers as he wrapped his arms around her waist and lifted her into his arms. Beth cheered and Mamie squealed as he spun Olivia in circles, kissing her repeatedly on the mouth. When he'd settled her feet back on the boardwalk, he rested his forehead against hers. "I didn't like your letter."

She shook her head at her own folly, and he kissed her forehead. "But I forgive you. If you'll promise me something."

"What's that?" she asked, linking her arms behind his neck.

"That you'll stay this time. That Friday Harbor will be your home. Our home. Together."

"I promise."

"Good." He pressed his lips eagerly to hers and lifted her off her feet as he spun her one more time in celebration.

"Alright you two, you have your whole lives to make out on the boardwalk. Now come along." Beth motioned towards Olivia's luggage and Matt grimaced when he spotted the heavy suitcase.

Laughing but still dabbing away her tears, Olivia rubbed a hand over his back. "You did say you loved me, right?"

"That I did, Liv. That I did."

She kissed his cheek.

"But I'm never lugging this thing again."

Laughing, she nodded. "I think I can live with that."

He snatched her hand before she could walk ahead of him and kissed her tenderly on the lips once more. "And here?"

"And here." She affirmed.

"And me?" He asked.

"Always." Her kiss lingered on his lips before she smiled and hurried towards her grandmother and his mom. Looking back over her shoulder, he met her excited smile with one of his own. He finally had *His Olivia*.

« Epilogue »

"We have ten minutes until they arrive, Matthew," Olivia called down the deck stairs and waited until her husband appeared from down below before reciting their checklist.

"Drinks?"

"Check," he called over his shoulder as he set about lighting candles and lamps along the freshly painted deck.

"Food? Check," she answered herself. "Oh, did you remember to invite Jake and his new girlfriend? What was her name again?"

"Naomi."

"Ah, Na-o-mi." She penciled it on her list.

"And yes, I did." He walked towards her and grabbed her hands. "Calm down, Liv. Everything looks great. And everything will *be* great."

Nervously, her eyes darted from one table to the next. "You sure?"

Laughing, he kissed her sweetly on the lips. "Absolutely." His fingers brushed her knuckles and his thumb paused on her ring finger as he toyed with her wedding ring. He brought her hand to his lips and kissed her ring. "I love you."

Her anxious face relaxed as she slipped her arms around his waist. "I love you too."

"Everything is in place, the house looks fantastic, the food will be fantastic," He placed a hand on his chest proudly. "And you are fantastic. I don't think we could have a better party."

Giggling, she rested her head on his chest and both took a few minutes to look out over the lake. Olivia still woke up most mornings in disbelief of her new life. Her life with Matthew.

When she'd decided to stay in Friday Harbor, they were married a month later, despite her mother's shock and objections that it was too soon. But in Matt and Olivia's minds they'd loved one another most of their lives and there was no reason to wait. Bilbo and Mamie retired to their small cabin in the woods not far from Matt's parents. And the property Matt owned, right in between the two, became her new home. Olivia now owned Anchors Aweigh, and Beth was her star employee, mostly covering Saturday mornings so Olivia could sail the first orcas tour with Matt. It'd become their tradition. They also sailed a few times a week, making sure to give Matt the taste of ocean that he needed. Used to living on the water, their latest project had been an adjustment for him. For the last eleven months he and Olivia had patiently overseen the building process on their first home and tonight was the unveiling of the finished product. She loved it. She loved him. And the only regret she had was not moving to Friday Harbor sooner.

"I think they're up here." Beth's voice drifted up the deck stairs and as she cleared the landing, she greeted them with a proud smile. "Look at you two enjoying your view."

Olivia regretfully slipped her arms from around Matthew, but immediately smiled as she wrapped Beth in a welcoming hug. "Thank you for coming."

"Of course. A housewarming party is right up my alley. I brought some sangria." She beamed. "Roy's bringing it up. It's a bit strong, but I think you'll like it." She winked as her husband appeared followed by Ramsey and Reagan.

"Hi." Olivia greeted them all with hugs and accepted the flowers Ramsey handed her. "Thanks,

Rams." She kissed his cheek, the big man blushing as he shook Matt's hand.

"Beautiful place, Matt."

"Thanks. It helps that I married a designer."

"Doesn't hurt," Olivia agreed on a laugh.

Several more people climbed their way to the top of the deck and Olivia stood in awe at the life she and Matt shared: the people that loved them and embraced her as part of the Friday Harbor family, the friends that made sure the two of them didn't work too hard and miss out on fun times, and the house, their beautiful new home. The dream that she could be with Matthew and have a job she loved, was fulfilled. Fifteen years was a long time to wait for love, but for Matthew… She gazed over at him as he animatedly talked with his friends, his charming grin, his unruly hair teased by the wind. For Matthew, fifteen years was worth it.

Find out more about Katharine and her works at:
www.katharinehamilton.com

Social Media is a great way to connect with Katharine. Check her out on the following:

Facebook: Katharine E. Hamilton
https://www.facebook.com/Katharine-E-Hamilton-282475125097433/

Twitter: @AuthorKatharine
Instagram: @AuthorKatharine

Contact Katharine:
khamiltonauthor@gmail.com

ABOUT THE AUTHOR

Katharine E. Hamilton began writing in 2008 and published her first children's book, <u>The Adventurous Life of Laura Bell</u> in 2009. She would go on to write and illustrate two more children's books, <u>Susie At Your Service</u> and <u>Sissy and Kat</u> between 2010-2013.

Though writing for children was fun, Katharine moved into Adult Fiction in 2015 with her release of <u>The Unfading Lands</u>, a clean, epic fantasy that landed in Amazon's Hot 100 New Releases on its fourth day of publication, reached #72 in the Top 100 in Epic Fantasy, and hit the Top 10,000 Best Sellers on all of Amazon in its first week. It has been listed as a Top 100 Indie Read for 2015 and a nominee for a Best Indie Book Award for 2016. The series did not stop there. <u>Darkness Divided: Part Two of The Unfading Land Series</u>, released in October of 2015 and claimed a spot in the Top 100 of its genre. <u>Redemption Rising: Part Three of The Unfading Lands Series</u> released in April 2016 and claimed a nomination for the Summer Indie Book Awards.

Though comfortable in the fantasy genre, Katharine decided to venture towards romance in 2017 and released the first novel in a collection of sweet, clean and wholesome romances: The Lighthearted Collection. <u>Chicago's Best</u> reached best seller status in its first week of publication and rested comfortably in the Top 100 for Amazon for three steady weeks, claimed a Reader's Choice Award, a TopShelf Indie Book Award, and ended up a finalist in the American Book Festival's Best Book Awards for 2017. <u>Montgomery House</u>, the second in the collection, released in August of 2017 and rested comfortably alongside its predecessor, claiming a Reader's Choice Award, and becoming Katharine's best-selling novel up to that point. Both were released in audiobook format in late 2017 and early 2018. <u>Beautiful Fury</u> is the third novel released in the collection and has claimed a Reader's Choice Award and a gold medal in the Authorsdb Best Cover competition. It has also been released in audiobook format with narrator Chelsea Carpenter lending her talents to bring it to life. Katharine and Chelsea have partnered on an ongoing project for creating audiobook marketing methods for fellow authors and narrators, all of which will eventually be published as a resource tool for others.

In August of 2018, Katharine brought to life a new clean contemporary romance series of a loving family based in Ireland. The Siblings O'Rifcan Series kicked off in August with <u>Claron</u>. <u>Claron</u> climbed to the Top 1000 of the entire Amazon store and has reached the Top 100 of the Clean and Wholesome genre a total of 11 times. He is Katharine's bestselling book thus far and lends to the success of the following books in the series: <u>Riley</u>, <u>Layla</u>, <u>Chloe</u>, and <u>Murphy,</u> each book earning their place in the Top 100 of their genre and Hot 100 New Releases. In 2019, <u>Claron</u> was featured in Amazon's Prime Reading program.

Katharine has contributed to charitable Indie Anthologies as well as helped other aspiring writers journey their way through the publication process. She manages an online training course that walks fellow self-publishing and independently publishing writers through the publishing process as well as how to market their books.

She is a member of Women Fiction Writers of America, Texas Authors, IASD, and the American Christian Fiction Writers. She loves everything to do with writing and loves that she is able to continue sharing heartwarming stories to a wide array of readers.

Katharine graduated from Texas A&M University with a bachelor's degree in History. She lives on a ranch in south Texas with her husband, Brad, and three-year-old son, Everett.

Made in the USA
Columbia, SC
01 October 2022

68443138R00129